DEADLIGHT

First published 1968 by John Long Ltd., London
This edition published 1983 by Kilbrannan Publishing Limited, Brodick, Isle of Arran, Scotland.

ISBN 0 907939 07 4

Printed and phototypeset on the Isle of Arran by Kilbrannan Publishing Ltd.

DEADLIGHT

by

ARCHIE ROY

KILBRANNAN
Isle of Arran

Author's Note

The Tormore Circles exist just as I have described them but there is no Department of Cybernetic Studies at Glasgow University nor do any of the characters in this book exist.

John Marshall's discovery is conceptually possible since it does not infringe any scientific laws or raise any paradoxes, but for the reader's peace of mind it should be stated that it also does not exist — at least, not yet.

A.E.R.

Glasgow

For
Mercer and Ian

What is truth said jesting Pilate,
and would not stay for an answer.

FRANCIS BACON:
Essays of Truth

CONTENTS

1   Landscape with Nightmare

I switched off. The square of light fled to a bright point then faded into darkness.

Suddenly aware of the effort I had put in concentrating, I eased my cramped position. The pain in my ribs dragged sickeningly at my mind and exhaustion lay like a deadweight on my shoulders. My eyes burned and my sodden clothes stuck to my body. My ear still throbbed and the cut on my face was bleeding again.

Once outside in the corridor I watched the moonlight pale as butter flooding through the window. The rain had ceased. I remembered how the wet road had gleamed among the shadowy undergrowth of whin, with the sides of the mountains raising themselves up to the black skyline where dark clouds raced over the summit as if eager to blot out the moon. Down on the shore the sea had imitated all moonlit seas after a storm, with waves pounding whitely on the wet shingle, pushing at a black ragged line of seaweed.

So the storm's over, I thought. At least that one is — next one is scheduled to begin now and should be a real dilly. Casualties are expected to be heavy. I suddenly felt stifled and scared and triumphant and desperately tired all at once. The outside scene faded behind hypnagogic images appearing unbidden from my exhausted mind in a succession of accusing, scrambled, episodic, badly-edited movies that could not be switched off. I saw the accusing faces of men and women, old and young, whose faith I had shattered, the angry, gobbling faces of the politicians I had displayed as buffoons and liars, the blank, unknown features of law breakers, major and minor, legal and moral, from whom I had swept security. There was no order in the succession. As fast as one scene dissolved, another took its place. There were the faces of those I had killed, mixed with those of the sadists and pornographers to whom I had given an inexhaustible supply of stimuli.

9

Crowding in on these came scenes of cavemen, of mammoths and pterodactyls and primitive rain-soaked forests. New faces appeared, known to me: Johnny grinning and shaking his head mockingly over and over again while Laura wept; my colleagues posed nicely in groups, some sympathetic, most united in condemnation. So it went on.

I found myself shaking, my right hand pressed over the damaged ribs to try to ease the stabs of pain that hit me. All at once the visions faded, the moonlit scene outside the house becoming hard and real again. The utter conviction that there was nothing I could do now to alter the situation pressed down like an incubus on my tired mind and I knew that henceforth there was no hiding place but the grave.

2   End in Doubt

It began for me, though I didn't know it then, when Johnny entered my room that August morning about ten o'clock. He saw the map of North America spread across my desk with the file of airmail correspondence beside it.

'Joining the brain drain?' He sat down, placing a long iron rod with a handle attached to it across his knees. 'May I interrupt you?'

'You have,' I pointed out. I put down the blue air letter I had been reading. 'No, they wouldn't have me. Anyway, I'm one of those stay-at-home Scots. I sometimes think that preparing a schedule for a trip to the States is as bad as controlling a deep-space probe approaching Mars. Between your question "On what dates can I see you?" to someone over there and their answer, there's at least a week and then all the available dates have to be dovetailed with respect to the time *and* the money available.'

He seemed singularly unsympathetic.

'Written your paper for the Conference?'

'You know that's the last thing to do.'

'When are you off?' he asked.

'End of the week. I fly on Sunday to Los Angeles, or as we hardened travellers call it, L.A.' I pointed my pen at the five-foot long iron rod. 'What's that?'

He lifted it. 'Rather neat, don't you think? I had it made in the workshop. It's graduated in half-feet.'

'Why?'

'If there are any long sandstone slabs buried in the peat, this will find them.'

'I see. You're still hooked on those stones.'

'Yes.' Johnny stood up, the rod's sharpened point resting on the floor, his hands on the horizontal handle as if he intended driving it through the boards. 'Gives the book-loving scientist a healthy, outdoor exercise measuring old megalithic remains and wondering what the hairy blighters who erected them were up to.'

'Does Laura think that?' I enquired mildly.

'Absolutely. At least, what she says is, it could have been fishing.'

I looked at him. Twenty-eight years old, with fair curly hair and a strong rugby-playing type physique, he did not appear academic. But he was. Indeed he was. After a brilliant First in Physics he had chosen to do research in cybernetics in London before being invited to join the Old Man's group here in Glasgow. He had that spark, that elusive gift so few of us possess, of really original thought, coupled with an insatiable curiosity and the ability to work single-mindedly day after day, week after week, until everything in the problem jelled and the break-through was achieved. Possessing boundless energy, he had already a number of first-class papers to his credit and was fast becoming a scientist of international repute. If anyone was going to succumb to the brain drain, I felt, it would be John S. Marshall. There must be a good number of American institutions, I thought, that would cheerfully equip a laboratory as bait to catch him.

For some reason, he and Laura had become very friendly with me in spite of our ten years difference in age, and I was often in their flat in Hyndland or in the bungalow they had built recently at Boquhan, near Killearn.

'You're not going off on holiday now?' I asked.

11

'No. Not until the end of August.' He hesitated.

'I'm on to something I can't leave. If it comes off, Roger, it'll be big.' He frowned and seemed strangely uncertain. 'Perhaps too big'.

'What do you mean?'

He laughed. 'How dramatic can you get?' He struck a pose, one hand held across his forehead, and intoned, 'Man was not meant to meddle in such realms.' In a normal voice he went on. 'Forget it. Go off to America. Have a good time — not too good a time, mind you, and perhaps I'll have something that'll make your hair curl by the time you come back.' He was part way to the door when he turned. 'Are you leaving a list with Anne of the people you're going to visit?'

I nodded. 'As far as I know them. You know how it is, however. Walt at Stanford hears what kind of work I'm struggling to do and says, you must visit Hiram at Dearborn because he's just finished off that particular problem. Or words to that effect.'

Johnny grinned. 'Yes, I know. Anyway, have you got the current issue of *Cybernetic Abstracts*? I do wish people would put a card in when they lift something out of the library.'

'I dislike the implication, buster. I am not guilty. Try Olive. I think I saw it on her desk yesterday afternoon.'

He thanked me and left. I wondered what new line he was working on. Then Anne announced a student to see me and I forgot about it in the effort to persuade the student that if he adopted a really original approach and worked for the September re-sit, he might pass. The next few days were hectic. What with seeing to passport, visa, ticket, vaccination and other chores that complicate travel between Britain and the States, I had little time for idle chit-chat with my colleagues. On the Friday afternoon at the teabreak I did spend ten minutes talking to Johnny, among others. I thought he looked tired and abstracted. It was the last time I saw him alive.

I always enjoy visiting the States. Apart from the fruitful three-day conference at Stanford, where delegates from four continents described their work in exploring the last uncharted territory on this planet — the human brain — I made my usual circuit, stopping off at UCLA, Pasadena, Washington, Dahlgren, New Haven and Boston to renew acquaintance with researchers and sharpen my scientific wits. It wasn't all dedicated work, of course. American hospitality wouldn't allow that and I don't suppose I got to bed before midnight more than twice in the three weeks I was away.

It was raining when the BOAC jet from Boston landed me at Prestwick and I experienced again that curious let-down, dissociated feeling you get when you've spent a considerable period travelling thousands of miles at high speed through different time-zones and meeting a non-stop succession of people. When the coach finally deposited us at the St. Enoch Air Terminal, it was about 11.30 a.m. I collected my cases, left the building and hailed a taxi outside the Subway. I hadn't slept too well the previous night, managing at best a half-doze troubled by unwelcome idolonic productions in sterophonic sound and glorious technicolor from my overstocked subconscious. Many of the images were of past events I realised still carried far too much emotional charge.

I slipped the key into the door of my flat in Hillhead Street and unlocked it. The air smelled stale. Oh well, I thought, I can get Mrs. Morton to come in on Monday. I picked up a dozen or so letters and magazines from the small semi-circular oak table on the left of the hall and carried them through to the kitchen after depositing the cases in my bedroom. I looked at my wrist-watch. It was five to twelve. I decided against going up to the College Club for lunch. By the time I had put on the immersion heater, unpacked, read my mail and had a bath, it was almost one o'clock. I left the flat, walked down to Great Western Road and along towards Byres Road and retrieved the Armstrong-Siddeley from the garage where it had lain for the past month. After paying the bill I drove down Byres Road, parked the car at the foot of Great George Street and had a meal in one of the restaurants that have sprung up there in the past few years.

After coffee, I shopped in Byres Road, buying a *Daily Express* and a *Glasgow Herald*, a bottle of milk, cereal, cold meat, a pack of ham, bread, butter and eggs, then drove home. Among the mail there had been a new *Scientific American* and an *Analog*. I spent the remainder of the afternoon reading, had a light snack about six, then read or watched television until nine-thirty before going to bed, earlier than usual, to make up for lost sleep. Thus although I had been in Glasgow half a day, I had met none of my colleagues and so didn't hear of the tragedy until the following morning.

The alarm woke me at eight. Between cereal and ham and eggs I phoned Mrs. Morton. By nine I had left the flat and was walking over the hill towards University Avenue. It was warmer than usual for a Glasgow September, with the promise of a hot, sunny afternoon to come. Reaching the Department I ran up the half-dozen shallow steps, pushed open the glass door and crossed the entrance hall. The notice-boards with their familiar collage of multi-coloured papers bearing details of scholarships, seminars, examination results and time-tables gave me an absurd home-coming feeling. I climbed the stairs to the first floor and walked along the corridor to my room. Sitting down at the desk I had left a month before, I began working through the neat pile of envelopes on my blotting-paper. Three were publishers' autumn book-lists, others were requests from various organisations for lectures; some letters from fellow-workers in other establishments I added to the lecture request list for answering later. There was one crank letter of the type certain university departments seem to attract. The writer had read my book on automata and belaboured me for stating that it was more important for man to map the interior of his skull this century than to explore the planets. 'Man was not meant to meddle in such matters,' she admonished me. I grinned happily and remembered Johnny's self-deprecating use of the same cliché. A little pleasant surge of anticipatory excitement rose within me. I dropped the letter into the empty waste-paper basket (it is fatal to answer such epistles) and got up.

Outside Johnny's room I stopped, hand upraised to knock and wondered why I hesitated. Then I realised his name-plate no longer faced me. The four screw-holes where it had been attached remained raw and unfilled. I felt my face twist in perplexity. I knocked and waited. There was no reply. I retraced my steps, noting that the plates on the other staff doors were all present and correct. I decided I'd go downstairs and see Anne. This time as I crossed the hall I glanced at the 'In-Out' board where the names of the staff were displayed. My puzzlement deepened when I saw that Johnny's name was again missing. Almost automatically I noticed that George, Olive and the

14

Old Man were in while the others, including myself, were out. I pushed over my slide from 'Out' to 'In', crossed to the door labelled "Secretary and Inquiries" and knocked. In reply to the invitation to come in, I opened the door and entered. Anne and the Old Man looked up from the files they were consulting.

Sir Mark Douglas-Forrest, Professor of Cybernetic Studies, straightened up and ran a hand through his halo of white hair in a gesture that fooled only those who did not know him. You don't become a Nobel prize winner by being vague and ineffectual.

'Ah, Roger, so you resisted the temptations of the intellectual fleshpots. When did you get back?' I told him. He and Anne glanced at each other. To my surprise, the Professor sighed and Anne bit her lip.

'All right, my dear,' he said. He put the pale-green file he carried on her desk. 'We'll sort out that equipment order later. Roger, would you mind coming through to my room for a moment.' He turned towards the communicating door between Anne's office and his room. I followed him feeling more and more perplexed and out of it all. When we were seated, he essayed a few polite enquiries about my trip for a minute or two, but his heart wasn't in it. At last he sighed again, pushed aside the paper knife he had been toying with and came to the point.

'You don't know about John,' he stated rather than asked.

'No, sir.' I waited uneasily.

He nodded. 'Thought not. Sorry to have to tell you, Roger, but John met with an accident — a fatal one — about three weeks ago.' He paused. 'I don't know if I quite believe it yet, you know'. He shook his head almost in desperation. 'What a waste! What an appalling waste!'

I sat there. Finally I said 'How did it happen? Car crash?' Johnny had been a skilled driver but had liked travelling fast.

'No. It happened in Arran. He must have fallen over a cliff. Somewhere near Blackwaterfoot, I think. He was found at the foot of it.' Sir Mark rose and crossed to the window. He looked unseeingly across the trees and green slopes of Kelvingrove Park towards the massive red sandstone outline of the Art Galleries.

'But he wasn't due to go to Arran until the end of August,' I said stupidly. Sir Mark shrugged.

'He switched a week of his holiday to August. Laura's mother was ill and she went down to London to be with her. John went off to Arran.' He turned away from the window. 'He'd been working very hard up till then and said he needed a few days to think out the next step. So off he went. Six days later he was found dead at the foot of this cliff.'

I still couldn't accept it. I saw him again in my room so very much alive. What on earth could have happened to cause such an accident. I made one of those obvious statements people come out with when they're mentally off-balance.

'So the funeral was held while I was in the States.'

'Yes.' Sir Mark sat down at the desk again. His expression became even bleaker. 'It was damn bad luck. Her mother was so much better after five days that she phoned Johnny to say she'd return on the Saturday. Johnny died on Friday.' He raised his hands from the desk surface and shrugged. 'If she had come back a day earlier, Johnny would have left Arran the same day and would probably be alive now. Damn bad luck.'

I nodded. Sir Mark seemed to brace himself. 'Almost certainly Laura will get over it — by the time you've got to be my age, Roger, you realise that human beings are pretty resilient. Trite, but true. It takes time, sometimes a long time —' he saw something in my face and broke off. 'Sorry, Roger, I forgot.'

Yes, I thought, sometimes it takes a hell of a long time.

'I'll phone her this evening,' I said. 'There's really nothing one can say but I'll phone anyway.'

'There's one matter arising from John's death,' he remarked. 'Do you happen to know what he was working on before you left?'

'No, sir.' I told Sir Mark what Johnny had said about his research.

'I see. So you don't even know if it had anything to do with Project Rover?'

'What makes you think it had, sir?'

The Old Man frowned. 'I don't know for sure. He did say before he went off to Arran that we might have to think again about the Project.'

'Surely not at this late hour?'

'I don't know. That boy had a really remarkable brain. He could have been on to something of first-class importance. The trouble is he gave no details. Said he had to go over everything again before he could talk about it. Quite proper, of course.'

I agreed, knowing my own reaction whenever I think I've discovered something new. After the first sense of elation, you think: 'I suppose it's all been thought of before — and published.' So you search the literature and if you don't find it you wonder next what's wrong with your train of reasoning. Only after checking and double-checking do you finally convince yourself that you've produced something worthwhile.

'What about papers, sir?'

'Laura very kindly gave me permission to go through his desk and files but there was nothing germane. It was quite a task. He wasn't the most legible writer in the world, as you know.' He paused. 'There was an incredible amount of stuff in his notebooks — some of it I recognised as material he subsequently published; a lot of it consisted of ideas, speculations, comments in quite a few scientific fields — many were doubtless blind alleys but a number had been developed to an extent that indicates we should do something about them someday.' Sir Mark rubbed one side of his face. 'But nothing I could see that referred in any new way to Project Rover.'

'I'm sorry, sir.'

'No, no Roger, that's all right. It was just a remote possibility that something he had said to you might give us an inkling of the nature of his researches.' He rose. 'Now, I'd better go next door and try to straighten out that filing tangle with Anne.'

He paused at the communicating door. 'I seem to spend more and more of my time in administration these days. I suppose it's a sign of age. Incidentally, I suppose you'll be giving the Department a report on your visit?'

I nodded.

'Good, then at tea this afternoon we'll arrange a time and date that suits everyone. In the meantime, why not go along to the lab. George and the technical staff have been building some toys they want to show off.' He smiled. I thought that for the first time in my ten years with him he seemed tired, almost frail.

The main laboratory ran most of the length of the ground floor, with small stockrooms and workshops opening off it. A staff of four technicians helped to design, modify, build, tear down and rebuild the wide range of apparatus and machines we found it necessary to have to further our research. There were the usual workshop tools — lathes, vertical drills, grinders, welding equipment, plus the usual electronic gear such as avometers, cathode ray oscilloscopes, power packs, amplifiers, wave generators, a microphotometer, a medium fast, medium capacity computer and a flexowriter enabling us to prepare tapes for the university KDF9 computer. A good proportion of the able space, however, was taken up by the rather unorthodox and usually untidy creations in glass, metal and plastic we had dreamed up in our efforts to get Project Rover off the ground.

I opened the glass door leading into the laboratory. Olive and George were down at the far end; with two brown-coated technicians named Black and Morrison, they stood around a piece of equipment I hadn't seen before. George, a clipboard in his left hand, pipe in mouth as always, was scribbling down notes. There was a tape-recorder running and as I approached I heard a not-quite-human voice recite a long string of nonsense syllables.

'Step up the gate by 10 per cent and repeat the run, Bill,' Olive suggested. George looked round as I joined them. He clipped the pen to his board and nodded.

'Hullo, Roger, when did you get back?' His plump, genial face, surmounted by a pepper-and-salt crewcut, gave him a pseudo-transatlantic air, heightened by his habit of wearing bow ties. Although the kindest of men, he often irritated his colleagues to the limit of endurance by his adolescent judgements on politics or philosophy and by the air he gave of a not too competent actor hamming up the part of the deep, pipe-smoking, cerebral scientist. Yet he had a brilliance amounting to genius in handling anything even remotely connected with electronics and could produce out of our lash-ups the most elegant, efficient circuits I have ever seen.

Olive Keydell was a trim, dark-haired attractive woman of about thirty. She had joined the staff three years ago when it became obvious that the work required a psychologist. She seemed happy and interested enough in the project though I sometimes suspected she felt her talents were being wasted probing into the elementary and fragmentary mental fields of our creations. Or perhaps she was finding of late that her heart just wasn't set on being a career girl.

I told them I'd had a talk with Sir Mark and how shocked I'd been to learn of Johnny's death. As we talked, I couldn't help noticing that in three weeks they had become relatively detached about the tragedy. The conversation finally turned to the new piece of hardware.

'Not a mobile one?' I asked.

'No,' said George. 'It's built to test the multi-level memory system we were talking about before you left. We've beefed up the number of units to ten to the fifth.'

'I see. With ten microsecond action times that should make its store effectively of order ten to the eight. Uh-huh.' I considered. 'How well does it perform?'

Olive looked almost approvingly at the squat, washing machine-sized object. 'We've run the usual battery of tests. Memory half-life, reinforcement rate, confusion — it exhibits nicely both retro-and post-active facilitation and inhibition and at least fourth-order conditioned responses. At present we're playing about with the mean setting, trying to get the best trade-off between above-threshold memory and error density in the recall.' She favoured me with one of her rare smiles. 'I think that if it attended a year of your Ordinary Class Lectures, it might pass the Degree exam quite comfortably.'

'In fact, a promising student. What's in its memory at the moment?'

'Oh, the usual nursery rhymes, some novels, number tables — oh, and Hamlet. Switch it on, George,' she ordered. Pushing back a stray lock of dark hair, she turned to me. 'Go on: it's fed by an all-octave receiver.' George flipped a selection of switches. A pattern of lights came on. I glanced at him and addressed the mike.

'To be or not to be . . .'

'. . . that is the question,' the not-quite-human voice took up. It proceeded with the soliloquy, making few mistakes as far as my hazy memory of the play could check. We all grinned at each other like fond parents at a school concert. I cut it off and tried other cues. It responded successfully to them all. I found that it knew 'Mary had a little lamb.' I recited to it a number of times 'Mary had a little lamb, some roast potatoes, apple tart for dessert and a cup of coffee' then cued it with 'Mary had a little lamb.' The machine continued '. . . its roast was white as apple and everywhere that cuppy went, that lamb was sure to go.'

'Not bad,' I said.

'We also finished the latest mobile one, Dr. Arnott,' said Morrison, the senior technician. 'It's somewhere around. It answers to the name of Dozey.'

He yelled the name. There was a whirring noise and along the passage there came trundling what seemed like a black, animated vacuum cleaner without the handle. It approached us almost ingratiatingly, a miniature television camera on its top revolving like a small radar scanner.

'Find Olive,' George ordered. The machine hesitated, buzzed like a hive of bees then came towards Olive, stopping about ten inches from the toes of her shoes.

'The pattern recognition unit must be fairly discriminative,' I said dryly.

'It is.' George's lips twitched. 'Go and plug yourself in at the wall, Dozey,' he ordered. The automaton whirled about and rolled away towards the far end of the laboratory. On its way it passed a bench carrying oscilloscopes just beyond which a cupboard stood. To the foot of the cupboard someone had attached at floor level a large mirror. Dozey's scanner caught sight of its reflection. It halted before the mirror as if fascinated.

'Oh, you gorgeous creature,' it said in a sexy voice, 'do you come here often?'

I knew what they had done, of course. The automaton's own pattern gave a signal that triggered off a small tape-recorder carrying the message.

'You ought to be ashamed of yourselves,' I said, 'using S.R.C. funds to build toys.'

'Actually,' Olive remarked, 'We'd better dismantle it. The other morning, one of the cleaners was in here. She was standing in front of that mirror when Dozey happened to approach. He saw his reflection, of course, but the cleaner thought he was talking to her. She fainted.'

George took pity on the mechanism, still trying to date itself, and ordered it to go to its kennel. With what sounded remarkably like an electronic sigh of unrequited love, it continued up the passageway to the far end of the lab, where it sidled into a rabbit-hutch-like enclosure and found the specially shaped power-point it used for sustenance.

We spent the rest of the morning in the lab talking over various aspects of the researches the Department was engaged on. Most stemmed from Project Rover, our attempt to create a class of mobile, self-repairing, adaptive, medium-intelligent automatons that could be sent as crew in deep space explorations to the outer planets of the Solar System, where transit times were measured in decades and where surface conditions were viciously hostile to life. Such robots would also be able to explore the ocean depths. As a bonus, the design and study of these automatons was shedding light upon the mechanisms of the human brain.

The work had been proceeding now for six years under grants from The British Science Research Council and the American National Aeronautics and Space Administration during which time we had gone from moderate optimism through despair at ever succeeding, to confidence that within another three sessions it would be all systems go.

About twelve-fifteen George and Olive and I left the Department for lunch. It being out of term, there were few students on the grass at the flagpole enjoying the sunshine, and the Club contained a quarter of the number usually found at that time of day during term. Since it was so late in the summer most faces had their share of sunburn. Sitting over coffee afterwards in the lounge I noticed the familiar groups were all represented — mathematicians up in the corner, engineers opposite the windows that looked on to the grew square of professors' houses, the bridge table in a window corner with four enthusiasts intent upon their devotions. The usual remarks came from passing colleagues: the Director of the computing laboratory in gently chiding tones to a companion:— '. . . but you do appreciate that the procedure would waste machine time . . . ', a forthright astronomer to a philosopher:— 'the crux of the matter is that the supreme merit of the steady state theory is that it *can* be disproved. . . ' It wasn't all shop-talk, of course.

The majority of conversations were doubtless concerned with politics, holidays, books, plays, golf, families, etc.

After lunch I dictated letters to Anne until three-thirty, a task I dislike though I retain a childish pleasure in receiving mail. At tea in the library we arranged a time and date (Tuesday at two-thirty) when the staff would hear my travelogue. Before the tea-break was over, Clark Desmond of Caledonian TV phoned. He wanted to discuss an idea for a scientific programme and invited me to have dinner with him in town one night. I chose Friday. Sometime around four-thirty the Extra-Mural Department phoned to settle the dates on which I would be taking my share of a course in 'Aspects of Modern Science' the following winter.

About five o'clock I signed the letters Anne brought me and decided to call it a day. I hadn't yet settled into a research frame of mind — that usually takes two or three days to achieve after an absence of a few weeks — but I'd broken the back of the log-jam of correspondence I'd found on my desk and in my flat. In any case I was in no mood for thinking deeply.

Going downstairs I put the mail in the out-tray in Anne's room and left. After high-tea in the Club — which was almost deserted — I walked across the hill in the warm evening sunshine to the flat. I washed, went into the lounge and reluctantly picked up the phone. After dialling I listened to the distant burr-burr of the call, conscious of a faint desire that it remained unanswered. It didn't. Laura's quiet voice repeated the number.

'This is Roger Arnott, Laura. I just got back from the States and heard about Johnny. I'm terribly sorry.' We form words on such occasions, I thought, that simply appal us with their banality and can only hope that they convey the real feelings that remain so inarticulate. By a quirk of the mind I remembered Johnny once telling me that at his wedding-reception he had tested the hypothesis that people assume on such occasions that the right words are being used and therefore pay no attention to them. At the usual congratulatory line-up of guests, he murmured benignly into several ears as their owners shook hands: 'I dismembered my grandmother this morning.' To his delight the usual abstracted reply was 'So glad' or 'A very happy occasion'.

Laura's voice was calm and yet pleased and again I was forced to remember that it had all happened over three weeks ago.

'Roger! How are you?'

'Very well. How are you?'

'Not too bad. I suppose I'm still buffered by shock.' Her tone was flatter now. 'It still seems a bit like acting a part in some monstrous play.' Her voice broke momentarily. 'It's worst when I wake in the morning.'

'I know. It does get better, Laura — it takes a long time but it does get better.' I didn't tell her that years later, when you think it's finally over and memory is drained of emotion, a stranger in the street, a laugh, can still rip the scar and sear the mind once again.

'Somehow I know that but at the same time don't believe it.' She hesitated. 'Roger, I must talk to you. If I don't I think I'll go mad.' I caught the thread of hysteria in her voice and uneasiness swept over me. 'You'll probably think I'm being quite irrational, that the shock of Johnny's death has put me out of my mind but I've still got to talk to you. I think I could accept his death if I knew it was an accident but I don't. I believe he was killed, Roger.'

The phone suddenly felt soapy with sweat. I spoke without thinking.

'Look, Laura, can I come out and talk to you?'

'Please do.' The entreaty in her voice was pitiful.

'This evening?'

'Yes.'

'All right. I'll be out about seven-fifteen.'

'Thank you, Roger. Even if you don't believe me, at least listen to me.'

'I will. See you then.'

I hung up, my mind whirling. Was she so disturbed and shocked that she was weaving fantasies about Johnny's death? If so would it be possible to dispel them by talking? Could there in fact be anything of reality in them? Oh, don't be ridiculous, I thought. Baffled and feeling a pressing sense of urgency, I left the flat. Two minutes later I was driving the Armstrong-Siddeley along the Great Western Road past the Botanic Gardens. The sun was still bright, though low, and I pulled down the visor to shield my eyes.

It was a beautiful evening and in other circumstances I'd have appreciated the journey out past Strathblane with the green and brown slopes of the Campsies rising smoothly to my right. But not this time. Beyond Strathblane, I took the right fork. I glanced at the dashboard clock. It was only seven-five. Eight minutes later I was slowing prior to turning up the little side road at Boquhan where Johnny and Laura's house stood among a dozen more bungalows scattered most attractively in completely unspoilt surroundings of fields and woods. As the wheels of the Armstrong-Siddeley crunched over the gravel and I brought it to a stop before the steps I found myself half-expecting the front door to open and disclose Johnny, clad in the shapeless sweater and grey flannels he affected at home. The door did open then and I breathed quickly and irrationally but the smaller figure of Laura stood there. At first glance she seemed unchanged, but by the time I'd climbed the short flight of steps, I saw that her face was thinner and paler and somehow tighter, the pallor emphasised by the black pullover and black stretch pants she wore.

'Roger, this is good of you.' She led the way into the lounge. A small log-fire was burning in the wide stone fireplace. The large picture-window in the next wall gave a magnificent view of the sunlit Lomond Hills. I felt a sudden and futile spurt of anger and resentment that she and Johnny had had their future shattered so irrevocably. It happens, I told myself, it happens all the time.

'You're looking very fit,' she said. 'All that nice American tan.'

I took the seat she indicated and came directly to the point.

'Tell me about it, Laura,' I said. 'Remember that I know very little about it, except that it happened while you were down south.'

'All right,' she said. 'I'll try to make some sense for you.' She drew on the cigarette she had lit. After a long pause she began speaking, a bit disjointedly at first, then more fluently. At times she seemed not to see me or even to be talking to me but to be reviewing events in an effort to assess them, to order them more rationally.

'I think it really began even before you left for the States, Roger. Johnny started working on something — I recognised all the signs, his abstractedness, the scribbling on bits of paper, the mooning about in the garden after dinner or working non-stop in his workshop till the

24

early hours of the morning, his fits of sheer agonised frustration when it just wouldn't come right.' She paused, her brows wrinkled. 'At least I'd seen it all before in lesser degree but never to this extent. I'd go off to bed night after night leaving him here in the lounge or in the workshop and maybe at two or three a.m. he'd come through to the bedroom absolutely exhausted.' She looked suddenly stricken. 'One night he said apologetically: "This is a hell of a way to treat you, darling" and I said I was used to it but if it went on much longer I'd seriously consider looking for some amusement elsewhere. He laughed — he knew I knew he had to finish off this work, whatever it was, before his mind would let him live normally.'

She paused again. 'Then, two days later, I detected a change in him. Before, he'd obviously been up against some formidably difficult research problem that had been baffling him, consuming every mental energy he possessed. Now, he seemed at the same time surer and . . . less sure.' Laura moved restlessly. 'Oh, I'm not making sense. What I'm trying to say is that he seemed to be solving his problem and yet, at the same time that I could detect his excitement at being within sight of success, I could see a certain . . . ' she passed her left hand over her forehead as she groped for words '. . . a certain uneasiness, almost a growing fear.'

'Did he tell you what he was working on?'

'No. This wasn't unusual. Sometimes he did, sometimes he didn't. Even when he did, it didn't always mean he thought I'd understand it or that he had any damn silly notions that talking over his work with his wife would increase our "togetherness". He felt sometimes that trying to tell me what he was after often helped him to straighten out his thoughts.' She tossed her cigarette into the fire and added a couple of logs from the brass box beside it. They shot hissing jets of sparks into the air.

'Anyway, one night he came into the bedroom. It was about three a.m. He'd been in the workshop all evening. Poor lamb, I remember during dinner thinking he was in absolute agony to get through to his work. I wasn't asleep — I had been, but I wakened. He didn't put the light on, of course, but went over to the window and stood looking out, his hands clasped behind his back. It was quite light — it was an absolutely clear starlit night. I watched his face. It seemed completely empty of emotion, of any expression at all. For a long time he stood there. Then he turned his head. I can remember his words clearly.

' "Are you awake, Laura?"

' "Yes", I said.

'He turned back again. "It's finished. One way or another."

' "What is it, Johnny?" I asked.

'He sighed, a great shuddering sigh that suddenly made me aware that he was almost drunk with exhaustion. "Don't ask me just now. I've got to think about it. *How* I've got to think about it. No, it's just too dangerous — " And then, Roger, he added: "Yet, can we afford to do without it?"

'After that he broke off and said no more. He came to bed and,' she hesitated, but went on honestly, 'he took me into his arms but not as a man takes a woman — he was a little boy wanting his mother to comfort him and give him security. Roger, he was scared, really scared.

'We fell asleep like that. Some time later I woke again. He was out of bed and putting on a pullover and trousers. He slipped out of the room and was gone about an hour. I lay wondering whether to get up and go to him or to stay where I was. When he came back he fell asleep and seemed to sleep quite peacefully.

'It was the next morning that a neighbour of my mother's phoned to say she had been taken ill the previous night. You know Mummy's been babied all her life, firstly by her parents then by Daddy. I'm afraid both Johnny and I know that—knew that—Oh God! it's very difficult, isn't it?—anyway, we decided that I'd go down to Mother's for a few days. Johnny said he'd go off to Arran, that he'd a lot of thinking to do and that he might as well get some fresh air. He added: "I can try out the new probe on the Machrie Moor circles." A strange look came into his face. "It may well be the last time I'll use it." He spoke slowly, almost as if what he said surprised him.

'He phoned the Tormore Hotel — you know it; it's quite small and by chance there was a cancellation — .' Laura gasped and her eyes filled and I knew it had suddenly struck her that if there hadn't been one to be found, Johnny might never have gone. She recovered. 'We packed and he drove me into the Central Station before he set off

26

for Ardrossan. That was the last time I saw him alive. Each evening after dinner for the next four days, he phoned from Tormore to see how Mother was. On the fifth night he didn't phone. I wondered a bit but didn't really worry, of course, though in fact I wanted to tell him that Mother was so much better that I would be coming back with her to give her a week's rest here.'

Laura hesitated and drew a long shivering breath. 'The next morning I phoned the hotel at breakfast time. They were a bit evasive at first, then revealed to me that Johnny hadn't returned for dinner and in fact hadn't been in all night. I didn't know what to think. I was alarmed, of course; the Moor is pretty isolated and you could be in difficulties if you broke a leg. I didn't get any satisfaction from the other end. I hung up after listening to their reassurances and spent the morning feeling terribly helpless, wondering what to do and telling lies to Mother. Just before lunch they phoned — I had given them the number— to tell me that Johnny had been found lying at the foot of Drumadoon. He was dead.

'Everything seems dreamlike after that. I was encapsulated by shock and sedatives and so I suppose that's why I was able to get through the next week, to make arrangements about Mother, travel north to Arran, identify the . . . body, be interviewed by the police — they were unbelievably kind, you know — and make other arrangements about the funeral . . . and so on. Sir Mark and Lady Mary were wonderful to me.'

'The police didn't think an inquiry was necessary?'

She shook her head. 'No. As far as they could see he had gone to the Doon, ventured too near the edge and fallen over. It's a sheer drop to the shore. They said there've been a number of deaths by accident of visitors climbing in the mountains of Arran. They don't appreciate how difficult some of the terrain is.'

She spoke evenly, obviously watching to see how I was taking this. I was conscious of a distinct feeling of dissatisfaction growing in me. Certainly climbers have died in Arran before now. The Castles, Cir Mhor, A'chir Ridge and Ben Bharrain are all traps for the unwary but Johnny hadn't been a climber. In any case, the Doon is not a climb. It is a rising headland covered with coarse grass and heather that on the south east slopes easily upwards; the only source of danger lies in the sheer drop of two hundred feet or so down to the rocky shore on the north east side. But only a fool would go so near as to chance slipping over. And Johnny was no fool. I also wondered what he had been doing up there. It was about four miles from the Tormore Circles he had been working on, more from his hotel. He had had his car, certainly, so the distance was nothing, and of course the Doon is of interest since it was once a Stone Age fortress — the ancient ramparts are still visible in their ruined state.

I suddenly remembered there is one large standing stone on the summit but it is nowhere near the precipitous edge. And yet, I reflected, how can we be sure what a person will or will not do. An idle stroll to the edge, a sudden dizziness and it happens. Then I recalled what Laura had been telling me about his state of mind and a rather unpleasant thought nudged at my mind. I tried to choose my words carefully.

'Those phone calls he made to you each evening, Laura. Was there anything in them that seemed . . . out of place?'

Something came and went in her eyes as if I had asked the right question. 'I think so,' she said quietly. 'The first night Johnny phoned was the evening of the day he arrived. He asked after Mother, hoped I'd had a pleasant journey, told me he'd a very comfortable room, that the weather seemed settled and that next morning he'd take his things out to the Moor and begin on the Circles. The conversation was much the same the following night, except that he told me he'd spent most of the day at the Circles.'

'Did you ask him about the work he'd been doing here?'

'Yes, I did. I asked him if the Arran air had enabled him to do his thinking. "Oh," he said, "I've thought and thought all right, Laura. There's plenty of time for that when you're out by yourself on the Moor with only the stones to keep you company". And his voice became so heavy and dull that I was sorry I'd asked. "But no joy, darling, no joy. The more I think about it, the more my mind simply yaws and rolls from one decision to the other." I asked him if I couldn't help at all, even if only to listen while he argued it out. He laughed but without any humour in his voice. "I don't think so, Laura. I wish you could, but this one I'm stuck with." She lit another cigarette, inhaled deeply and continued. I noticed her hand was shaking.

'That was the second night. On the third, he said, "You know, I'm beginning to think the Ministry of Works has suspicions I'm trying to run away with their megalithic circles. Several times today I'm sure I've seen two men watching me through glasses from the other side of the Machrie Water. Or maybe they're policemen and they think I'm one of the Great Train Robbers digging up some of his loot. What a place to bury it, eh? In a four-thousand-year-old stone cist." He wished me goodnight and I hung up.

'I didn't attach any importance to the incident then. In fact, the following night I joked about it, expressing surprise that he was still free to phone me. He didn't rise to the invitation to spin me an impossible tale as he usually did. Instead he quickly turned the conversation to an inquiry after Mother's progress and for the rest of the phone call I got the impression that he was abstracted and worried but was trying not to show it. That impression has nagged and nagged at me ever since.'

She frowned and gazed into the fire, her arms hugging her knees, then looked up at me. Her face was bleak and chilled. 'I never spoke to him again.'

She rose. 'That's all, Roger. Think about it while I go and make some tea.' With that she left the room. I let myself sag back in the armchair. The thoughts and feelings that came to me simply increased my depression, my sympathy for Laura, my confusion. The dark possibility that had occurred to me still claimed my attention. Laura's account of Johnny's state of mind before he went to Arran and during his short stay there suggested that suicide could not be ruled out. He wouldn't have been the first scientist or scholar who had broken his mind on a too-tough problem, realised his mental power had been crippled, and taken his own life in a fit of morbid depression. But I wasn't sure. It somehow did not seem like Johnny. Again I visualised his strong features as I had last seen them. I found myself shaking my head. Could he have really developed some new discovery he'd made to the position where he had to decide whether to publish it or suppress it? But if so, what? What would really scare Johnny in these days of

29

hydrogen bombs, nerve gases, and lethal bugs to the extent that he spent weeks in a state of the jitters? And what the hell had he meant when he'd added: 'Can we afford to do without it?'

I thought of something else. If he had spent so much time in the workshop, what was he doing — writing or building? If the former or both, why had Sir Mark found nothing when he examined Johnny's notebooks? Did he take the stuff to Arran with him for safe keeping? I rubbed the back of my hand across my mouth as thoughts chased each other through my mind. I was beginning to agree with Laura to the extent of feeling that there were things here requiring an explanation. And just then I realised that if Johnny's mind hadn't snapped, his story to Laura that he was being watched also required an explanation.

I rose to my feet and crossed to the wide window. It was still light though the sun was very low by now so that the hills and trees cast long shadows. They matched the multitude of doubts in my mind. I tried to separate the accident from Johnny's work. If there had been nothing anomalous about his behaviour before he'd left for Arran would we not simply accept his death as one of those tragic, heartbreaking fatalities that occur again and again, smudging out a talent the world could ill-afford to lose? I thought of Pierre Curie and the wagon in the Rue Dauphine, of young Moseley meeting the sniper's bullet in Gallipoli. Had Johnny simply slipped over the cliff-edge? Had it crumbled under him? I just didn't know. Crossing the room, I entered the long hall that led to the kitchen.

A stifled gasp stopped me abruptly at the open kitchen door. Through it I saw Laura standing by the cooker. As she waited for the electric kettle to boil, another sob escaped her. I saw that her cheeks were wet. Again that gust of anger shook me. She looked up and passed the heel of her hand over her cheek.

'Sorry, Roger. I won't be long.' She poured boiling water into the already prepared teapot and transferred it to the tray carrying cups, saucers, plates, some cake and biscuits. I picked it up and carried it through to the lounge. After we were both supplied with tea, I questioned Laura.

'No,' she said, 'there don't seem to be any papers in the workshop concerning his project. Sir Mark went through them.'

'So he told me. But you know yourself, Laura, that when you're working on something that lasts for days, as this did, we can fill scores of sheets of paper.' I remembered then that Johnny, like many scientists, had the habit of dating the quarto sheets he invariably used with the year, month and day, followed by the sheet number in that day. A look at his notebooks — in reality loose-leaf folders — should tell whether or not there was a substantial work output during the period in question. Of course, if he had had doubts about publication, he might conceivably have burnt the work. I suddenly recalled Laura telling me that he had left the bedroom for an hour the last night he spent at home. I hesitated.

'His things would be brought back from Arran, I suppose?'

'Yes. I put them in the spare bedroom. Why?'

'I wonder if he took the missing work to Arran.'

A little more life seemed to animate her. 'It's possible,' she admitted. 'I just haven't been able to bring myself to go through the books and other things he had with him, Roger. Do you want to look at them now?'

'In a few minutes, if I may. And I'd like to have a quick look at his notebooks too. Did Sir Mark take them away?'

'No, he came out one day and studied them. They're in the workshop.'

'I'd like to see it too.'

She gasped. 'I forgot, Roger. It seemed so unimportant beside . . . everything else. On top of everything, the workshop was burgled a week ago.'

'Burgled?'

'Yes. I found the next morning that the window catch had been forced. But as far as I could see, nothing had been taken or damaged. I called the police, of course. They didn't hold out much hope of catching the burglar.' She sighed. 'I can't say I care very much whether they do or not.'

'Did the Old Man go through the notebooks before or after the burglary?'

'Before.' She looked at me. 'Oh, I see. You thought the burglar might have removed the worksheets.' She put her cup and saucer down. 'Does this mean you think there really is something more than ..... that Johnny's death was not an accident?'

I found myself putting out a hand to stop her. 'No, Laura, don't misunderstand me. I just don't know — I'm still trying to grasp the situation. Tell me, have you told anyone else about your feelings?'

She shook her head slowly. 'No. The police in Arran asked me about Johnny's state of mind — I think I said that apart from being over-tired, he was quite normal — at the time I was so numb with shock that I just didn't think of telling them that he'd been watched.'

Or said he had. I got to my feet. 'Could I have a look now at the things Johnny had with him?'

Laura rose and led the way along the corridor into the spare bedroom. It was decidedly colder there and the slightly musty smell told me that the room hadn't been opened since the miscellany of books, maps, a steel tape, pens and pencils, a clip board, a writing pad and other objects lying on the bed had been placed there. Conscious of Laura's mute presence just inside the door, I hurriedly sorted through the varied gear. Two of the books were science fiction, the third was *The Book of Arran, Volume I*; the maps consisted of a six inch to the mile Ordnance Survey of the Machrie Moor area and the one inch to the mile map of Arran. The clip board still held some papers. Four were covered with figures, phrases and pencil sketches that I recognised as referring to the geometry and dimensions of megalithic remains. But no message, no cryptic symbols that spelled out the word 'clue' for me at any rate.

'Can I see the workshop now, please?'

Laura turned and left the room. After a last glance at the objects scattered over the bedspread, I followed her, my feeling of uselessness sharper.

The workshop should have been the other spare bedroom but Johnny transformed it, running shelves around its cream walls, putting a broad, bench-like table in its centre and a desk over by the window. The shelves and tables held test-meters, amplifiers, semi-cannibalised surplus electronic gear, cathode ray oscilloscopes, an electric soldering bolt, and other gadgetry. Three shelves on the left-hand wall acted as a bookcase for over a hundred technical books on a variety of subjects. As I stood there, my nostril caught the faint metallic reek of solder clinging to everything.

There was an angle-poise lamp on the desk, plus the usual equipment of blotter, pencils, pens, ruler, paper-clips, a small black case of drawing instruments, one or two standard reference books, including a *Kaye and Laby*. There were no work-sheets. I glanced at Laura.

'Sir Mark returned the notebooks to the filing cabinet.' she said. I opened the first drawer and began a quick search. Fortunately Johnny, in spite of the Old Man's comments about his handwriting, had been systematic so that the notebooks were adequately labelled with year and subject tackled in that year. I was not so much concerned with the actual contents of the pages as with the run of the dates at the top of the pages. I opened the current notebook at the back. The last date was July 24th. Six sheets, labelled Roman fashion, held that date. They dealt with a feedback problem that had been giving us trouble in a Project Rover mechanism. I spent ten minutes making a rapid search of the earlier notebooks in case Johnny had nodded and put more recent worksheets into them by mistake. But there was nothing.

I straightened up and looked round the workshop. It was two months since I'd last been in it with Johnny but I have a reasonably accurate visual memory. I could see that certain pieces of apparatus had been shifted but I was unable to discover anything new, even when I wandered round the room.

'Let's go back to the lounge, Laura.'

She nodded. Her face was pinched and chalk-white.

When we were seated once more, with fresh logs on the fire, she turned expectantly towards me.

'Well, Roger?'

I hesitated; then told her what I'd found, or hadn't found. She leant forward almost eagerly, a faint flush relieving the pallor of her face.

'But he worked and worked that last fortnight before he went to Arran. Not only at his desk but also building. I *know* this was so, Roger!' In emphasis her fist hammered down on the arm of the couch. 'And I just don't see him falling over that cliff. He wasn't stupid!'

No, I thought, he wasn't. But he could have burned his papers and broken up any apparatus he had put together and he could have committed suicide — or simply and by sheer accident tumbled over. Not for the first time in my life, it was brought home to me how uncertain is our understanding and knowledge of events. Koestler was dead right, I reflected. We drift through life like sleepwalkers. I tried to be honest with Laura and at the same time reassure her and transmute her feelings into a calmer mode. Among the things I pointed out was that if it had not been for his spell of overwork with its enigmatic conclusion, the accident would have been accepted as just that.

'But the men following him,' she put in. Ah yes, I thought, another point; real or — ?

'Again we can't be sure, Laura.' She looked at me, her whole attitude proclaiming her feeling of desertion and I knew with a sense of dismay that I wasn't getting through to her.

'Laura,' I asked very hesitantly, 'do you want to talk to the police again?'

She shook her head miserably. Even she realised there was nothing concrete she could tell them. Then her eyes met mine and it was her turn to hesitate.

'Roger, is it at all possible that Johnny took the papers with him and they are still down there?'

'It's possible he took the work with him,' I admitted slowly. 'In fact I can see that he might have wanted to go over it again — but surely all his effects were brought back by you?'

She sighed. 'I thought I gathered them together but in the state I was in . . . Roger, please. I know this is a lot to ask but could you — would you go down there and make sure?'

Oh, God, I thought, what she really wants me to do is to go down and look for anything suspicious. The papers are only an excuse. Even if Johnny took them with him he wouldn't mislay them so that they'd be left there. And yet again I knew I wasn't sure. If there was the slightest chance of finding them, I also knew I had to try. But as for snooping around — I didn't even know how to begin.

'All right, Laura. I'll go down. I'll see the hotel people and have a word with the police.' Her look of gratitude made me add hurriedly — 'But I can't promise a thing.'

'I know, Roger.' She rose as I stood up. 'I feel a little better now, having talked to you about it. You will keep in touch, won't you?' I assured her I would. Outside the house it was quite dark now, though a faint light to the west still outlined the hills against the paler sky. At the foot of the steps I turned and looked back at Laura's slight figure framed in the lighted doorway. Once in the Armstrong-Siddeley, I switched on, turned on the headlights, waved once again to Laura and drove away, my mind resembling a stockpot of emotions, speculations and re-runs of sequences from her story. I usually enjoy night driving but on this occasion most of my attention was directed inwards while I zombied along the dark winding road towards Glasgow.

I drove up Hillhead Street about ten-thirty. In the flat I put on the lounge radiator and wandered about, reliving the evening. My thoughts, if anything, became gloomier and more unsettled. On an impulse I switched on the TV set. The late news was just finishing. The South African situation had evidently taken a further predictable step towards bloody disaster. The commercials followed. An exquisitely-dressed young man practically wet himself with enthusiasm over the deodorant qualities of a new soap he had discovered, holding it up before him like the Holy Grail. I switched off and went to bed. It was a long time before sleep came.

3   The Sleeping Tide

Twelve hours later I stood at the rail on the top deck of the *Glen Sannox* car ferry as it throbbed its way across a ten-mile stretch of water between Ardrossan and Arran. Ahead, the island's blue-tinged mountains presented their spectacular panorama, with the tent-like shape of Goat Fell at their centre. I noted the familiar hump of the Holy Isle sheltering Lamlash and further north, the sweep of Brodick Bay towards which the motor vessel's prow was aimed. The weather still seemed settled, the sea was dead calm and the bright sunlight acted as a detergent on the whiteness of the wake rolling away behind the ship's blunt stern. Arran in September has always had an attraction for many people, so that there were several hundred passengers on board the ferry though none, I suspected, with a mission like mine.

Sir Mark had surprised me earlier that morning when I had phoned him at his home. I had told him about my visit to Laura and about the lack of any worksheets during the relevant period. I had also mentioned her request to me to visit Arran and check that they hadn't been left there. Sir Mark seemed to attach more weight to her suggestion than I did. Or perhaps he felt that the sooner she could be convinced there was nothing to explain about Johnny's accident the quicker she'd recover. Anyway he thought the visit certainly should be made and suggested one or two courses of action. I rang off, then phoned British Railways Enquiry Office at the Central Station to check that I was in time for the morning boat. I packed a holdall and within twenty minutes of my brief conversation with the Old Man, I was driving the Armstrong-Siddeley down Byres Road towards the Clyde Tunnel. At Winton Pier, Ardrossan, there was no trouble in getting a place for the car in the ferry which was a relief since it secured me my own transport once I arrived in Arran, without the need to hire a car there.

The *Glen Sannox* began its broad run into Brodick Bay that would end at the white-painted pier and I left the warm, teak rail, prior to going downstairs to the car-deck. All around me other passengers were making their first, anticipatory gathering together of cases, rucksacks, golf-bags, fishing-rods and all the other gear the island's visitors bring to it. I joined the line of car drivers and their families descending into the lower deck, finally settling myself behind the wheel of the Armstrong-Siddeley amid a general noise of slamming car-doors. A minute later the vibration and hum of the turbines changed pitch in response to the telegraphed command from the bridge. There was a period of comparative quiet as the ship sidled up to the pier before the engines reversed and the ferry was finally warped in. I reached deck in the fourth load raised by the car lift and followed a duck-egg blue Hillman Imp down the black steel ramp on to the pier where a stream of passengers with their luggage made for the pier exit gates. At the car

36

exit I slowed down and handed over my six shillings pier-dues to the man with the polished leather satchel slung across his shoulder.

Once across the busy pierhead area with its cars and buses, I turned right towards Brodick. Ahead of me the road stretched through the village, the houses and hotels lying on the left, the shore and sea bordering the right. Half a mile further on, the shore with its wide, sun-sparkled sandy beach and neat row of red, green, white, brown and blue bathing boxes swept round to the far right below the lower green slopes of Goat Fell. The brown-walled castle stood there gazing out over the bay where sailing dinghies and other light craft moved like pond beetles over the water. When not in swimsuits, the majority of holidaymakers wore the traditional Arran uniform, old sweaters and navy-blue or khaki shorts for the men and blouses, slacks or shorts for the women. I found myself noting that the girls' short shorts had finally reached the maximum limit of curtailment.

I was a boy of four when my parents first took me to Arran on holiday. We stayed in Brodick in a cottage just across the road from the beach. We went back year after year for the best part of a decade. I recalled the extreme attachment I had developed for the smooth cinnamon beaches, the rock-strewn, sparkling rivers, the olive and brown hills and moors, the sharp, bluish-gray ranges with names as arresting as their soaring ridges — Ben Nuis, Ben Tarsuin, Ben a' Chliabhain, A'Chir Ridge, Cir Mhor, Caisteal Abhail.

I remembered the red deer on the hills, the chalky sheep scattered everywhere one went, especially the tame sheep of Corrie that came to you for titbits and begged on their hind-legs. Brodick didn't seem to have changed much since I was last here. The road was wider and the village hall seemed to have been extended. There were some new cottages on the left as I drove past the Golf Course, but the great flat megalith — the Stronach Stone — still stood in brown dignity as it had done for almost four thousand years, pointing to the Sleeping Warrior Range.

At the signpost, I turned the car left and began the climb over the String Road, one of the only two car routes slashed across the body of the island. As I reached the summit and turned down to the Machrie side of the island, I glanced over to my right across the glen where a herd of twenty to thirty deer were grazing just up from the old road. One of those childish superstitions that never quite leave us even if we do know them to be quite irrational nudged me and I caught myself wondering if the White Stag had been seen lately.

A few minutes later, at the foot of the String, I turned right on to the Machrie Road. At one point in the road, where the land falls away to the south-west in rolling peat-moors, I coud see in the distance the black, pencil-like shapes of the surviving stones of the Tormore Circles, standing like the last living members of a cavalry unit besieged by Indians. On the far horizon, almost due south, the land, from being reasonably flat, swept up to the right to form the plateau leading to Drumadoon.

I was now nearing the sea, approaching it downhill and obtaining as I did so a synoptic view of the Mull of Kintyre stretching out along the western horizon, at its nearest some seven miles away, across the Kilbrannan Sound. Passing the Machrie Hotel, I put the car on the coast road for half a mile before turning right into little Glen Tormore. It is only a few hundred yards deep with one small, mountain-cold stream falling straight down it out of the green bowl of the corrie at the head of the glen. The Tormore Hotel stands at the mouth of the glen in a couple of acres of ground, a pleasant white-washed, sturdy house of some dozen bedrooms, usually frequented by fishermen and those looking for the quieter holiday.

The main gate was open so I drove the Armstrong-Siddeley up the drive and into the yard at the back. Turning off the ignition I sat and considered my next move. Someone inside me jeered at me and I studiously ignored the names of several well-known fictional detectives I knew I bore absolutely no resemblance to. With a little spurt of anger, I overcame my reluctance to move and got out of the car.

Half an hour later I was seated at a small table in the dining-room having lunch. There were eight other tables, all with their complement of guests, ranging in age from three to seventy-odd, most sporting varying degrees of sun-tan and informal attire. After the meal I meant to have a talk with the proprietor then visit the local police. If time permitted, there were one or two things I could do that I honestly didn't think would be of any use whatsoever.

After lunch, I went upstairs to the room I had taken for one night and waited until I was sure that the hotel staff would have had their meal. I then returned to the office with its frosted glass partition and knocked on the door. A dark-suited, bronzed man in his forties with flat, black hair was seated at a desk holding account books and bills. On the wall above the desk were pinned the usual merchants' calendars, bus and boat time-tables. I also noted a faded photograph of a Spitfire with a group of young men in RAF uniform standing before it. As I entered the room, the man at the desk glanced up.

'Well, Mr. Arnott, isn't it? What can I do for you?'

'You're Mr. Fullerton, the proprietor?'

'Yes. Nothing wrong, I hope?'

'No, no. I wondered if you could spare me a few minutes just now.'

'By all means. Always glad to get away from these damn books. Have a seat. Now then. . . ' He looked expectantly at me.

I had rehearsed my story and had decided to stick essentially to the truth. I told Fullerton I was a colleague of Dr. Marshall's; that we were looking for some of his work-papers and that we weren't sure whether he had brought them to Arran, or, if he had, that his wife had recovered them. In her state she couldn't be sure of anything — Fullerton nodded in understanding — and so I'd been sent down to ask if anything had been found.

'I'm afraid you're on a wild goose chase, Mr. Arnott. As far as I know, nothing was left behind. If it had it would have been handed in to me.' He paused, his face sober, 'Ghastly business. You know, that sort of thing somehow hits you harder than the deaths you've seen in action. I suppose it's because you don't expect it. And yet, accidents do happen. Still, that's no consolation, is it?'

I seized the opportunity to ask him about it. He was in no way reluctant to talk about it but I learned nothing fresh. Johnny hadn't come in to dinner, had been out all night, his wife had phoned next morning, mild alarm had been felt and then his body had been found at the foot of the Doon.

I couldn't think of anything else to ask. After a pause, Fullerton spoke again, his pencil drawing circles on a scratch pad. 'It certainly put a bit of a damper on the guests. He was very well liked. A bit quiet, you know; seemed at times to have things on his mind, but then, who hasn't these days.' He threw down the pencil. 'Look, I'll ask the wife about this — if you don't mind — though I'm quite sure it'll be useless.' He left the office, returning a minute later with the pleasant, motherly-looking woman I had seen when I arrived that morning. She too had nothing for me. She seemed genuinely distressed at recalling the event.

'That poor lamb,' she said, 'coming all the way from London to find her husband dead. They've no children, have they?' I shook my head. 'I don't know whether that's a blessing or not,' she went on. 'I'm really sorry we can't help you, sir.'

Her husband stirred. 'Just a thought,' he put forward hesitatingly, 'and probably a damn silly one; but if he had those papers on him when he fell over the cliff, could they have fallen out of his pocket and still be lying there. Or been picked up and turned in to the police by now?'

I supposed it was possible. It was hardly probable but worth looking into. I thanked them both and after a few minutes of more general conversation, left the office. After making sure the One Inch Ordnance Survey map was in my pocket, I took the car down the drive. Once out of Glen Tormore I turned south onto the coast road and continued past the Machrie village hall and golf course. Crossing the bridge over the Machrie Water, which I noticed was running too low for the tastes of fishermen, I drove until a little sign indicating Balnagore appeared. For a moment I wondered whether to leave the car and walk, but a memory of Johnny saying he usually took his car up to the Circles decided for me. I opened the barred iron gate, drove the Armstrong-Siddeley through it, then got out and closed the gate before taking the car in low gear up the cart-track between fields dotted with sheep. The deeply-rutted lane was dry and just wide enough to take the big car and I hoped it wouldn't deteriorate any more as I progressed higher into the moors. By now the fields were left behind, the road snaking through brown-black peat-banks crowned with tufts of bell-heather.

Some time later the long bonnet of the car dipped as it reached the top of the last rise and I stopped and drew on the brake with its gentle ratchet sound. Before me the whole of the area known as the Moss was spread out for miles in every direction, its surface of peat, of heather, bog-cotton and broom a coat of many colours. Away ahead in the distance, beyond the Shiskine Road and the green cultivated fields, the mountain slopes swept up parabolically, their heights enhanced by the supreme clarity of atmosphere a fine Arran day on the Machrie side always seems to produce. Much nearer, a matter of a few hundred yards away, stood the Tormore Circles.

Over to my left a stone outlier, pointing like an admonitory finger to the sky, poked through a grassy mound; across to my right, what looked like a ruined cairn could be seen, its great slabs tossed about as if some giant had been rummaging inside it. Some way ahead, the cart-track petered out beside another mound bearing a double circle of massive granite blocks.

I started the car and ran it slowly downhill and across to the end of the peat-road, its springs creaking reproachfully. In fact I now saw that the road still continued beyond the blocks at least a little way out on to the Moss but was not, in any stretch of the imagination, of any use to a car. I also noted with mild surprise a red Mini Cooper standing down beside the ruins of two cottages.

Turning the Armstrong-Siddeley off the track, I got out and climbed the low grass-covered mound until I stood at the centre of the double, concentric circle of standing stones. I recognised it from Johnny's graphs. About forty and sixty feet in diameter, with eight and fifteen blocks respectively, the circles were, as far as one could see, still as their builders had left them three and a half thousand years before. Behind me, on a slightly higher hill, one solitary stone rose; ahead of me, two hundred yards to the north-east, an enormous sandstone slab some thirteen or fourteen feet tall marked the position of another circle. About the same distance further east, three survivors quite as large showed where yet another circle had stood. Far beyond the single stone, the two ranges of hills bordering the Moor met to the north-east in the vee-shaped valley of Glen Eisbeg.

I suddenly remembered Johnny saying that the builders had laid out part of their system of circles so that if you stood where I now was and looked beyond the circle marked by the single survivor, up through Glen Eisbeg, then on midsummer's day you saw the Sungod rise there.

On the other hand, if you walked to that circle and looked up at the hills in the direction indicated by the circle marked by three survivors, you were looking in the direction the Sungod rose at the spring and autumn equinoxes. In this way, he went on, these people bound together calendar-keeping for seed time and harvest, and their religious festivals.

'They weren't savages, Roger. A section of them at least could count, could design and carry out difficult engineering feats — some of these stones must be twenty-two feet long by five by two feet and weigh at least ten tons.'

I looked out over the Moss and tried to imagine life in those days, almost four millenia ago, two hundred generations of men away from us. From air photos in Johnny's possession, I knew that apart from the stone circles, the Moor was covered with dozens of hut circles; the whole area must have supported a largish community of fishermen, hunters and primitive farmers. And at night, the only illuminations would be stars and moon and the fires before the huts. No TV, no adverts, no pounding technology, no atomic bombs, no polluted and murdered rivers, no nerve and bacteria weapons, no jet-set, no purple hearts, no pop singers or film stars. Perhaps for the first time I began to appreciate the appeal these stones, the long cultural echoes of the ancient people of Arran, could have to someone like Johnny. My mouth quirked at the memory of how he had even set out in a part of his garden at Boquhan a model of the complex, on a scale of one inch to five feet.

Across the bright blue vault of the sky a high-flying plane drew a white contrail. I began to pick my way over the uneven moor where generations of peat-cutters and cattle have left a multitude of holes just made for breaking ankles. As I drew near the circle with one great slab still upright, I noticed a figure in red blouse and white shorts inside the three-stone circle. She was carrying a tripod with camera attached. By the time I approached it was set up to her satisfaction and she had the camera trained on the largest grey sandstone slab which must have exceeded fourteen feet in height. I recognised a girl who had been in the dining-room at the hotel. I am no good at estimating women's ages but I guessed she was about 26. She was most attractive with shortish dark, curling hair that just avoided being black, was medium-tall with a very nice figure neither model-thin nor yet peasant-thick like those of some champion tennis-players. Steady blue eyes fringed with long dark eyelashes looked out of a lightly-tanned face, producing an impression of a well-integrated and basically friendly personality. She can be serious, I thought, but undoubtedly she has a sense of humour. I smiled at her and said 'good afternoon' in my best voice.

She smiled in return. 'Hullo. Can you help me?' Her voice was low, yet warm and pleasant with a standard English accent.

'How?'

'Well, I want to get a picture of this big fellow here, against the background of Ben Bharrain and I've just realised that the size of the stone would be best indicated by having someone stand beside it.' She grinned, revealing excellent white teeth. 'Would you?'

'By all means. But if the camera's all ready, would it not be better if you showed me which knob to press while you stood beside it?' I didn't add that I thought she'd undoubtedly be more photogenic than I would. She shook her head.

'That's nice of you but I've got far too many of those already and it becomes a bit of an embarrassment to show my friends — you know, "me beside this" and "me beside that" and "Oh look, there's me again beside the other" '.

I went and stood beside the great moss-covered slab while she took her picture. I only hoped for her sake I had neither of my usual photographic expressions on my face, the 'Man that is born of woman hath but a short time to live' one or the 'Bugs Bunny sparkling teeth' one.

'They're very impressive, aren't they?' I said, running my fingertips down the warm, rough stone.

'Yes, they are.' She did things to the camera before unscrewing it from the tripod. 'Do you know anything about them? Everyone I ask down here says brightly that the Druids put them up but I have the feeling the Druids are blamed for much too much.' She began to telescope the tripod.

I told her what I knew about the Circles. She listened with genuine interest.

'You've made quite a study of them, haven't you?'

I disclaimed all expertise. 'A friend of mine was the expert here.'

'Was?'

'Yes. How long have you been staying at the hotel?'

She put the tripod in its plastic case. 'I came down last Saturday.'

'Then the accident must have happened to John before you arrived.'

Her head moved about one inch. 'You mean . . . ?' She looked straight at me now and I noticed how cobalt-blue her eyes were below the dark brows. 'He was the man who fell over the cliff?'

'Yes.'

She frowned. 'I heard about it from some of the other guests who were here at the time. He was a close friend of yours?'

'Yes.'

'I'm sorry.' She swung the plastic case across her back. 'But why are you — ?' She broke off, raising each arm in a sketch of a shrug. 'I'm sorry again. None of my business.'

I smiled. 'Don't apologise.' I took my hand off the slab and straightened up. 'I suppose you could say I'm down here on a million-to-one shot. In any case, I want to talk to a few of the people who were here when John was here. I'd give a lot to know — ' It was my turn to break off.

The blue eyes gazed straight into mine.

'What?'

I looked away to the coast. 'It was such a stupid accident. So utterly unlike him.'

'Tell me about him,' she invited, 'if you'd care to.'

Somehow I found myself accompanying her back across the Moss, trying to describe Johnny to her. It was quite ridiculous — I didn't even know her name. Almost as if she read my mind she said: 'Look, my name is Claire Stewart.'

'Mine is Roger Arnott. But your name, and accent? Do they go together?'

She laughed. 'Scottish two generations back but educated in England. Don't hold it against me.'

We came up the slope to the double circle and she indicated the Armstrong-Siddeley. 'I see you brought your own transport.' Her head came round and she regarded me thoughtfully. 'What do you hope to achieve down here?"

I did my bread-cast-on-the-waters stunt again, telling her about the missing worksheets, about the possibility that they had been handed in to the police or were still somewhere on the Doon or at its foot. And said again I wanted to see some of John's fellow-guests if there were still any in the hotel.

'There should be,' she murmured. 'I suppose you're off now to see the police?'

'That and one or two other things.'

She was on the verge of replying when her attention was caught by a third car coming over the peat-road at the last rise. She turned back to me.

'Look, Mr. Arnott, you'll be in to dinner tonight, won't you?' I nodded. 'Well, if I may I'll think about what you've told me and try to find out who were here when the accident happened, and,' she smiled, 'if I may, I'll join your table for dinner.'

Almost before I could agree rather dazedly, she was away, striding down the slope to the red Mini Cooper. By the time the Sherwood green Zephyr Six had bumped its way up to the double circle, the Mini Cooper had swung round and was ready to circle the bigger car before starting off back along the road. By that time I had thought (a) is she avoiding the other car? (b) if so, why? (c) it's quite a new twist, the girl inviting herself to have dinner with the man, and (d) why does she make such an impression on me?

I shrugged and turned my attention to the occupants of the Zephyr, a man and a huge, brown-black Alsatian dog that looked capable of snapping off a standing stone with a casual bite.

The man stood for some seconds gazing after the red Mini Cooper, then he turned towards me and I saw that it was yet another person who had had lunch in the hotel, namely the one with the grey, pointed beard and clever if somewhat petulant face. He carried a heavy walking stick and as he approached I noticed the deep tooth-marks about the middle of the stock. The dog, obviously possessed of a superfluity of energy, pranced around him, its salmon-pink tongue hanging sideways from its open mouth. The man threw the stick as far

45

as he could and it curled through the air with the dog bounding over the moss in pursuit.

I exchanged greetings with the newcomer.

'I see you're driving an Armstrong-Siddeley,' he said. 'Marvellous cars. Pity they stopped making them.'

I agreed. He had a precise manner, as if he weighed each word or phrase mentally before delivery.

The Alsatian brought back the stick and laid it at its master's feet in invitation. He picked it up and threw it away again before turning to me. 'I don't know who gets more exercise this way, Bran or myself.' He indicated the double circle of granite boulders we stood beside. 'We often come up here. These stones are like old friends. Do you know anything about them?'

'Not a lot.'

'Well, this circle's called Fingal's Cauldron Stones. The giant Fingal put his cooking-pot over these stones and lit a fire underneath. At least, that's how the legend goes. While the meal was cooking, he tied the leash of his dog Bran —' his eyes twinkled as he saw me glance involuntarily over to the Alsatian — 'to one of the stones. That one over there, in fact.' He pointed to a boulder in the south-west sector of the outer circle. 'Let me show you the "evidence" '.

We approached the stone and he indicated a hole about two inches in diameter cut right through the granite. 'The leash was tied through there.' He straightened up. 'I often wonder what the real purpose of that hole was. It's quite obviously artificial.'

'Perhaps a leash to make sure that the sacrificial victim didn't get stage fright at the last moment.'

His mouth twitched. 'Perhaps. Are you staying long at the hotel?'

'A day or so. And you?'

'Oh, I don't stay there though I occasionally have a meal there. I live in Carradale House.' I looked at him with fresh interest. Carradale House stood on the other side of the little stream running down Glen Tormore. Situated in a dozen acres of wooded land, it was an impressive brown sandstone example of well-to-do Victorian architecture. When I was a boy it had belonged to a shipping-firm family with numerous offspring, who had kept a respectable number of motor-launches and sailing dinghies in the little stone harbour on the shore. The family had grown up, the world had changed and for many years the house had been shut up. In my simple way I was glad it was being used again. I said as much to him.

'Oh, no relation to the original owners, I'm afraid. The house belongs now to Mensana — the physical fitness people. You've probably heard of them.' I had, vaguely. 'We placed this branch in the west of Scotland for a number of reasons. It's out of the way — no major distractions to seduce our guests away from the regimen. And we got it reasonably cheaply. Who else would want a huge house on an island these days. And there's walking, climbing, fishing, boating. All healthgiving and restoring to the jaded businessman. And yet it's extraordinarily near Glasgow. We usually bring our people across in the *Glen Sannox* but we also have a large launch and can land a helicopter from Abbotsinch if necessary in the grounds.' He threw his walking-stick again for the tireless Alsatian. 'I am the House Director and Warden, you might say.' He smiled in a self-deprecating way.

'Since you knew the house in the old days, perhaps you'd care to come along while you're here and see what changes we've made in it? By the way, my name is Kenneth Leighton.' He held out his hand. It was firm and dry. I gave him my name.

'I'd certainly like to see over the house.'

'Excellent. What about tomorrow morning? It's a quiet day, Sunday.'

We settled for ten o'clock. He bent to pick up the stick and I found his eyes glancing up. 'By the way, I saw you talking to our celebrity.' He enjoyed my bewilderment for a moment before continuing. 'You didn't know? That was Claire Stewart, the authoress.'

I had read one or two of her books. She wrote rather good historical novels and documentaries wherein she really created and brought to life the period in question without having to rely on the almost mechanical stage-setting of some historical authors. Her insight into human nature was remarkable and I remember enjoying in particular *Through A Glass Darkly*, a highly successful reconstruction of the era of psychical research when Sidgwick, Myers and the other founding fathers were at work struggling through the late Victorian morass of prejudice and superstition.

'Are you sure? She seems very young.'

Leighton grinned. 'I know. I rather like her books and had assumed Claire Stewart must be forty, at least. But that's her. Rather off-putting, don't you think?'

'Why?'

'Well,' he said, smoothing back his greying hair, 'I'm not taken with brainy women. I like them decorative. Though she certainly is damned attractive.'

Yes, I thought, you like them to be suitably impressed with your own brainpower, don't you? Leighton glanced at his watch.

'Well, I must be off. There are some people coming to the House this afternoon that I must prepare for. I'll look forward to seeing you tomorrow.' He called for the dog and they got into the Zephyr. I watched it turn and bump along the peat-road until it vanished from sight over the rise.

Now that I seemed to have the Moor to myself at last, I wandered from circle to circle in a long circuit that brought me at length to the top of a peat-covered hill on which a single stone rose, overlooking the double circle. From this vantage point the whole of the ancient system could be seen and quite suddenly my memory re-ran Laura's voice as she quoted Johnny's words. 'I can try out the new probe on the Machrie Moor Circles. It may well be the last time I'll use it.'

A cloud covered the sun and I found myself impatient with inaction. I descended the hill, swung myself behind the wheel of the Siddeley and sent it back over the track. Once out of the Moor I turned left towards Blackwaterfoot and Drumadoon. As I drove I tried to remember where the police stations were located. Brodick, Lamlash and possibly Whiting Bay. I could find out in Blackwaterfoot. I finally descended the last slope to the coast and a minute later was steering the car past the gravel parking area of the Blackwaterfoot and Shiskine Golf Club that lies between the beach and the Doon. A passable track for cars and farm vehicles runs beside the first tee, hugging the sandy coast for several hundred yards before turning inland. When Druma-doon Farm appeared I drew the car off the road and stopped. Getting out, I crossed two or three fields with scattered cows and black-faced sheep edging suspiciously away from me and began to mount the lower south-eastern slopes of the Doon. Soon I was passing between the tumbled ruins of the original stone-age battlements that with the precipitous drop on the north-west side of the Doon must have produced an impregnable position.

For the next twenty minutes I roamed about the plateau or wandered along but not too near the edge of the cliff that bordered the seaward side. The grey porphyritic rock forming the Doon outcropped all over the top in shelves and ledges or massive stone blocks five feet high in places. Between them patches of rough grass and heather tufts did their best to blanket the hard surface. I jumped down on to a broad ledge some twenty to fifty feet wide that ran along the edge of the sheer drop. Ahead of me across the Kilbrannan Sound the Kintyre hills were in sunshine. The buzz of an insect emphasised the silence. A growing sense of disbelief that Johnny could have been so careless as to fall off the top began to stir within me. I turned away, crossed the plateau and descended by means of a steep path along the flanks of the Doon that brought me at length to the shore.

Climbing over a fence I tramped over the shingle-banks at the foot of the great talus-slope of fallen rocks, out of which soared the enormous columns of rock forming the sheer vertical wall of the Doon, their tops about two hundred feet above sea-level. From weathered crevices all over the massive crag, sea-birds banked and climbed in random flight, their cries coming faintly to my ears as I gazed upwards at the crest. Any thoughts I had had of making a tentative search at the precipice foot for a packet of papers disappeared. The shattered columns of broken rock heaped in the slope at the base of the face produced a tumbled disarray providing a multitude of holes and cracks. My only hope was to find out the exact place Johnny's body had struck after its fall. I supposed that if I searched I might still find indications on the rocks. . .

I looked out to sea. The water, dappled with sunlight, the warmth of the pleasant late-summer day, and the dark background of my thoughts produced a strange impression of a benign countenance, behind which lurked something sick. Some words came into my head: '. . .such a tide as, moving, seems asleep, Too full for sound and foam, When that which drew from out the boundless deep Turns again home.' I shivered and decided it was time I visited the police. Once back at the car, I turned it and drove through Blackwaterfoot before taking the Shiskine Road leading to the String. The journey to Brodick took twenty-five minutes. The local policeman was out but his wife was helpful. She remembered the occasion and suggested that I went over to Lamlash to see the sergeant, who had looked after the case. I waited while she phoned to confirm that he was available, then climbed into the car once more.

The police station stood on the outskirts of Lamlash opposite the modern secondary school. Sergeant Mackenzie was in his shirtsleeves in the neat front garden, pushing a lawnmower over grass that seemed short enough already. He was a big, well-built man of about fifty, with thick, white, bristle hair cut short, that emphasised the tan of his square, capable face. As I approached the green wooden gate he straightened up and looked at me. He listened quietly while I told my story once more.

'No papers were found or handed in, Dr. Arnott. As far as I know Mrs. Marshall collected all her husband's property. I won't say it's impossible the papers fell out of his pocket when he went over the edge but I really think it unlikely. If the papers were loose and scattered as he fell, some at least would have been found. If not — .' He paused and I knew he was visualising the thousands of crevices in the talus-slope.

'Would it be possible to show me the place he struck?'

'Yes.' He looked at me. 'We can go across right now if it would suit you. I'm off duty.'

I accepted the offer, feeling uncomfortably that I was squandering his off-duty time unnecessarily. He went indoors to collect his jacket and leave word regarding his movements. Since I was staying on the other side of the island, we left in our separate cars. Less than an hour later, we were trudging across the fields towards the Doon.

'How do you think the accident happened?' I asked.

'We think he must have gone too near the edge and slipped.'

'Did you find the actual spot he went over?'

'We went up, of course, and examined the area above the place the body was found. There was nothing conclusive —.' He turned his head. 'Have you been on top of the Doon? Well, you'll know then that it could be extremely difficult to pick up any evidence that anyone had slipped over — unless of course we found any of his effects there or he happened to leave marks on a bare patch. There was nothing.'

He spoke carefully and thoughtfully and I noticed that he still had a ghost of a West Highland accent. I pressed on.

'Was there a fatal accident inquiry?'

'No.'

'But I thought in the case of a death that wasn't natural there would automatically be an inquiry.'

He smiled. 'Not necessarily. If the investigating officers are satisfied, there need not be an inquiry. A report may not even be sent to the Procurator Fiscal.' He paused at the foot of the Doon and looked at me. 'If fresh evidence turned up at some future date that aroused doubt, then the case could be reopened.' We climbed the fence. 'Did you know Dr. Marshall well?'

'I suppose so.' While the shingle crunched under our feet I tried to describe Johnny to him. He began to climb over the tumbled blocks of grey stone lying above high water marks.

'Yes, that's much the picture I gathered of him. Not a careless chap?'

'Anything but.' He nodded, his face impassive.

I clambered after him and wondered if he had any doubts and what his reaction would be if I related Laura's story to him. I supposed I should. In fact I edited it and told him about Johnny's feeling that he was being followed. The sergeant listened until I rather haltingly finished. As I did, he stopped and I realised we were at the top of the steep talus-slope, about eighty feet above the shingle banks. Two yards ahead of us the great columns making up the talus-slope rose sheer, carrying my gaze up their oppressive bulk to where the uneven crest made an overhead horizon with the blue of the cloudless sky.

The sergeant regarded me steadily as if assessing me. Then he sighed.

'Do you believe this story of Mrs. Marshall's?' He saw my hesitation and shrugged. 'You know, we did make as wide enquiries as we could. I talked to Mrs. Marshall, of course. It was my impression that she believed her husband was . . . under strain of some sort. Other people down here who had met him also agreed about that.'

'He had been working very hard.'

'Quite so.' So the police really used that expression, part of me marvelled. So usefully non-committal.

'We of course thought of suicide. It fits the few facts there are just as well as the accident theory. In some ways better.' His eyes held mine. 'But why cause more grief.' He dug a pipe and pouch out of one pocket and carefully filled the bowl before lighting it. His cheeks moving in and out regularly, he drew the match flame into the packed brown tobacco till it ignited. I had the feeling that he was choosing his next words with care.

'Neither of us has so far mentioned the third possibility, but it's in both our minds. Did someone do him in? Where sudden death occurs, Dr. Arnott, unwitnessed, or there isn't a wealth of circumstantial evidence to support accident or suicide, you must consider it possible, if however remotely, that murder was done.'

There now. Out in the open. I found myself taking a deep breath, a sudden picture before my eyes of the sunny panorama of sea and land surrounding us benignly while we stood there at the foot of Druma- doon, two tiny mortals discussing the sudden death of a third. The sergeant continued.

'There are human beings who like to kill. I don't really profess to understand their motives. Perhaps the reward is enjoyed in the act of killing; perhaps they get a thrill afterwards in realising that they have destroyed, snuffed out, a fellow human being and got away with it. Perhaps they dare God when they kill. See me. See what I do. I defy You. And they usually choose strangers as their victims.' He paused. 'The Moors murderers, Christie. How many don't we catch? And how many don't we catch because they forget each episode soon afterwards and lead a normal, useful life until the next time?'

That was a nasty thought.

'Now the vast majority of accidents like this one *are* accidents. But it is remotely possible that your friend was singled out by someone like the people I've been talking about, was watched, followed up to the top of the Doon, and pushed over. On the other hand, it is overwhelmingly more likely that he stumbled and fell or had some sort of brainstorm through overwork and pitched himself over.' I nodded, a cold lump of depression in the pit of my stomach. The sergeant was pointing to a slab lying at an angle against other jumbled prismatic fragments of fallen cliff.

'This is where the body was found. Judging by his injuries he must have died instantly.'

'Was his face — I mean, did Mrs. Marshall have — ?'

'Strangely enough, his face was undamaged. His wife identified him without any trouble.'

I turned away. He looked about him. 'Shall we try to find those papers, Dr. Arnott?'

We tried for the best part of an hour without success. Then we climbed to the top of the Doon by the path round the other side and cautiously searched the vegetation in the vicinity of the spot on the cliff-edge directly above the place the body was found. We had no more success. Calling it off, we walked back to the cars, morally certain that no papers lay there. I thanked the sergeant for his help, apologised for putting him to so much trouble and said goodbye to him.

'Not at all, Dr. Arnott. The search had to be made. Possibly I'll see you again some other time. Goodbye.'

He let in the clutch and drove off. I pressed the starter and followed in the Siddeley. At the junction I turned northwards on to the Machrie Road while the sergeant continued on through Blackwaterfoot proper. I reached the hotel fifteen minutes later. The time was ten minutes to seven.

4   Death Closes All . . .

Once in my room I crossed to the washhand basin and turned on the taps. I looked at my reflection in the mirror, rubbed my chin and decided to shave before dinner. The operation of wetting, soaping, lathering and razoring my face (old stone age Arnott) that usually helped me to think didn't work this time. I had no fresh ideas. I combed my hair, put on my jacket and went downstairs to the small bar where I passed the last fifteen minutes before dinner with a Bristol Dry. Finally the sound of the gong disturbed the surface of my moody thoughts like a pebble dropped in a pond and I pushed aside the empty glass I'd been toying with.

As I crossed the hall, Claire Stewart came downstairs in the company of one of the families I had noticed at lunch. She was dressed in a white-collared, electric blue silk frock that set off her tan admirably. She smiled and inclined her head.

'Hullo, Dr. Arnott. Come and meet the Mitchells.'

She introduced me to the parents and the boy and girl. Dad was a fit fifty with Mum some ten years younger and still attractively pretty. The daughter Elaine was at that uncertain age between girl and woman that immediately catches your sympathy; the son David was like so many first-year students I'd taught — impressionable, intensely idealistic, one hundred per cent honest, and convinced he was grown up. I felt very old. When we entered the dining-room and Claire Stewart accompanied me to my table, David stared icily at me before casting a look of such naked worship at my companion that memories of my own youthful first infatuation flooded my mind with a wave of compassion.

We sat down.

'They seem a nice family,' I offered as an opening gambit.

'They are. The kids are a bit energetic where tennis and swimming are concerned. I think they could go on all day.'

On an impulse, I said quietly: 'Let the boy down lightly.' She understood immediately. Her face solemn but her eyes sparkling, she nodded slowly.

'I will.' She looked mock-solicitously at me. 'Were you ever — ?'

'It happens to us all. It's marvellous — and shattering. There are usually no ill-effects, however.'

I noticed the proprietor, in light-fawn mess jacket, eyeing us speculatively as he supervised the table maids. It occurred to me again that my companion didn't seem to care a hoot for convention. To my surprise my gloom began to lift and I began to enjoy the meal. I wondered just how our relationship would develop. Even on such short acquaintance she intrigued me. As she talked and I replied, I found myself admiring the way her thick, dark hair framed her head, the way her slim, capable hands with medium-long nails would emphasise a point, the composure in her manner. She wore just a suggestion of eye make-up and her mouth, with its slightly full lower lip, looked warm and soft and I thought I knew just what it would feel like to kiss. A part of me watched my reactions with alarm. Again I recalled the remarkable maturity of her work and a desire to find out more about her came to me. I wondered about her background. Though she was extraordinarily attractive she wore neither engagement nor wedding ring. With a certain wry amusement I noticed she was very unobtrusively using the dodge of asking the man about himself and his work. Because she seemed genuinely interested I let myself be led pleasantly for a few minutes before deciding enough was enough.

'What about yourself? Someone told me this afternoon you are Claire Stewart, the authoress.'

Her mouth twitched in amusement. 'I am. Who told you?'

'A Mr. Leighton, who lives in Carradale House.'

'Oh yes.' For a moment she seemed to sit still and composed and I got the impression her composure was a facade behind which things happened. Then the moment passed and I wondered if I'd imagined it.

'And you're surprised?' she said in a resigned tone.

'Yes. And intrigued. I enjoyed your last book particularly — *Through A Glass Darkly*. You surely put an enormous amount of research into it.'

'More than I intended. Digging into diaries and old books, or pamphlets and private letters, always opens up interesting sidelines to seduce you away from the main object.' She laughed. 'And it's such a well-documented period. They seemed to spend half their lives writing to each other.'

'In resounding, Dickensian, Empire-building prose.'

'Too right, cobber!'

'Did you find your visit to Sludge-land revised your ideas about the wonderful world of psi?'

'In a number of respects.' I listened with interest to her words, my estimate of her intelligence going up and up. I have never subscribed to Leighton's view that intelligence in women is off-putting. If they remain feminine then their attraction is enhanced when the pleasant discovery is made that they not only possess a mind but that they are not afraid to use it. In any case the feminine slant on things is always fascinating. But in the main, our topics were kept relatively trivial and anecdotal until coffee. During the business of pouring coffee and hot cream into the small cups, she became thoughtful. Putting brown sugar into her cup and stirring, she said quietly:

'I had a word with the Mitchells this afternoon about your friend. They are the only ones now who were staying at the hotel when your friend had his accident.'

'Oh.'

'Not very helpful, I'm afraid. Like everyone else they were terribly shocked — because it was so unexpected, because he was young and well-liked, because he didn't seem the sort of person to be careless.'

'What sort of impression did he make on them?'

'Very pleasant, good-natured, interesting when they got him talking but he seemed a bit moody and thoughtful at other times. They said he went off for most of the day to the stone circles.'

'I see.' Or rather, I didn't see. There were still too many possibilities with no clear-cut evidence to support any of them. My mind wandered off on unprofitable speculations until I recalled it.

'Nothing else?'

She shook her head. 'How did you get on this afternoon after I left you?'

I summarised my afternoon's activities while she listened attentively.

'What do you think now?' she asked.

I shrugged. 'I don't. It's all terribly unsatisfactory but I suppose I can't do anything more.'

'It's a bit like the research I did for *Through A Glass Darkly*. More coffee?' She refilled my cup. 'All sorts of conflicting and misleading events turn up to obscure the motives of the people involved. You kept feeling that if only you could have had five minutes with them it would have all been sorted out.'

I nodded. On an impulse I said: 'Let me ask you an unfair question. If this situation turned up when you were researching for one of your books, what would you make of it?'

'In this case. . .' she hesitated, 'I think I'd have to admit defeat. The relevant factors are: Dr. Marshall's character, the alleged scientific discovery, the possibility of missing papers, the alleged phone calls and their content, his moodiness, the nature of the accident.'

'I notice you don't include the men following Johnny.'

'All right. But I must again prefix this factor with "alleged".' She bent her head and with the tip of her forefinger traced the rim of the saucer before her. Then she met my eyes. 'There's one theory that does fit everything. If he had a breakdown, destroyed his work and committed suicide, that could account for every factor. Including the irrational ones. Otherwise it doesn't make sense unless you drag in all sorts of other theories, much more improbable.' As she gauged my mood, she leaned forward. 'I'm sorry but there it is.'

I nodded unhappily. 'It's very much the conclusion I've been shying away from. But if that's what happened, it's so totally unlike him!'

'Well, I can't judge as you can. But can we predict what anyone will do when their mind breaks?'

'No, I suppose not.' I found myself biting my knuckle. 'What can he have been working on? It seems such a total waste if it is lost.'

' "Death closes all, but something ere the end,
Some work of noble note may yet be done". '

'Yes. Who wrote that?'

'Tennyson.' She smiled. 'It comes from a surfeit of endless banquets of Victorian literature.' She sobered. 'Perhaps your friend's judgement should be respected.'

'What do you mean?'

'Perhaps his discovery or invention or whatever it was was too dangerous to let loose.'

I looked at her. 'You'd have no pangs of conscience about suppressing knowledge?'

'Certainly not,' she shot back. 'Would you?'

'I don't know. I seem to change my mind about this from time to time. Fundamentally I'm against censorship — and suppressing scientific discoveries is surely censorship — but on the other hand I wouldn't show any fool how to culture up lethal strains of bacteria in his kitchen if I discovered a nice easy domestic way of doing it.'

'Well then — ?'

'I'd need to think about individual cases as they arose.'

'You feel your judgement would be adequate?'

'Hell, no! But it's the best I can do.'

'Perhaps this was the dilemma Dr. Marshall had to resolve.'

I mulled that one over. If I had filtered any sort of truth from the muddy water of speculations, second-hand accounts, impressions I had been presented with, it quite probably resided in that part of the matter. But it got me no further. I suggested we made a move and we rose from the table.

In the hall she said: 'I suppose you'll be going off in the morning?'

'No, probably in the afternoon unless I can think up any further enquiries to make.' I told her of Leighton's invitation to me to visit Carradale House. Again that strange veil-like expression descended over her face.

'Do you know him?' she asked.

'No, not really.' I explained how the invitation arose. She nodded. 'Should be quite interesting.'

By this time we had wandered to the open main door of the hotel. The evening sunlight enhanced the glossiness of her hair.

'When are you going back?' I enquired.

'In a week's time.'

'And where is "back"?'

She smiled. 'Glasgow.'

'Glasgow!'

'Yes. I lived in London near the British Museum while I was working on *Through A Glass Darkly* but since my next book has a Scottish setting, I thought I'd take a flat up here. I moved in in March. I'm really only getting everything sorted out now.'

Out beyond the hills of Kintyre the sun was still a good hour above the horizon. I turned back to her.

'Look. I certainly don't feel like calling it a day and I haven't been round the north end of the island in years. Would you care to drive round to Brodick with me? We could call in at the Douglas for a drink before coming back.'

Her eyes met mine steadily for a moment then she smiled.

'All right. Give me five minutes to get a cardigan.'

I fetched the Siddeley round to the front of the hotel and waited until she reappeared at the main door. She slipped into the front passenger seat and I closed the door with its usual well-mannered click. As I slid in behind the wheel she indicated the facia.

'Nice! Real wood. My Mini is certainly nippy but compared to this it's like a fox terrier beside a Great Dane.'

'Nicely put. I'm very fond of the old Siddeley. It's still in perfect running order so why should I replace it?'

'Why indeed.'

Still small-talk and exploratory skirmishing, I reflected with amusement as I pressed the starter.

Dougarie Lodge came and went, then Whitefarland Point, with its palm trees that bear witness to the mildness of the island winter. We passed through Pirnmill, Mid Thundergay and still were content with an occasional comment, so peaceful was the evening. When we rounded Coillemore Point into Loch Ranza Bay, the hills were casting deep shadows over the water and the ruined castle, slate-grey on its grassy promontory. The Armstrong-Siddeley began the steep climb up Glen Chalmadale. On our left, the ground rose sharply before falling down to unseen Laggan and Millstone Point where once a flourishing community fished and farmed, evaporated sea water in great stone troughs to recover the salt, mined coal, and carved out millstones for export. Not a soul remains.

Further down the Glen we passed North Sannox, another victim of the clearances. I pointed out the traces of former cultivation still visible on the hill slopes.

'Where did they go?'

'Mainly to Canada. Megantic County, near Quebec. You still find Arran names there today, McKillop, Sillars, Kerr, Fullerton, McKelvie. Do you know the Canadian Boat Song?'

'I don't think so.'

' "From the lone shieling of the misty island,
Mountains divide us, and the waste of seas,
Yet still the blood is strong, the heart is Highland,
And we in dreams behold the Hebrides." '
She looked out again at the green patches among the heather as the car followed the winding road down to the coast.

'To make way for sheep.'

'Ah, but you see, they stood in the way of progress and improvement—'

'Not to mention profit.'

We passed through much-painted Corrie, Sunday-silent in the twilight. When we entered Brodick ten minutes later, the western sky above the Glen Cloy hills was splashed prismatically with the crimson and gold hues of sunset.

After our drink in the Douglas's comfortably warm cocktail lounge, its lighting reflected in a hundred brightly-labelled bottles — what a twentieth-century contrast to the silent ghosts of North Glen Sannox — we came out once again into the night air. It was chillier now, the last pale light dying down behind the Brodick hills. The bay was quiet and still, the beach deserted, the fishing parties long since returned to hotels and boarding houses.

Once we had passed through the village I turned the car left on to the String Road. Occasionally the beams from the headlamps caught the amber eyes of a sheep huddled at the road-edge under the bank; once or twice a rabbit or other small animal left it almost too late to break the spell and bound off to one side.

'There's a sense of time suspended in travel like this,' she said. 'I feel neither tired nor alert. It must be because I'm the passenger and not driving.'

I glanced across at her, her face palely illuminated by the light from the instrument panel.

'I know,' I replied. 'The only effort arises in making the decision to stop when the journey is over.' Indeed I wished that the distance across the island was very much longer but even as I did so, the crest was reached and the winding road brought us down to the coast at Machrie. As the car crunched over the gravel before the hotel Claire sighed.

'Very nice. Thank you very much.'

'I enjoyed it. I'll let you out before I garage the car.' I got out and opened the offside door for her. We said goodnight and I watched her enter the hotel, her dark figure outlined against the hall illumination. In my bedroom I stood looking out of the window into the darkness for a time, without really thinking, a strange mood of mingled elation and uncertainty upon me, then smiled wryly and prepared for bed.

Going down to breakfast next morning I found to my surprise that Claire was sitting at my table again.

'Good morning,' she said. 'I'm afraid you'll have to blame Mr. Fullerton for not getting the message straight. He had set my place here.'

'I wouldn't dream of doing so,' I assured her. 'In fact, if I'd known, I'd have got up earlier.'

I looked out of the window. It promised to be another fine day. During the meal I learned that she was joining the Mitchells in a climb to the top of Goat Fell, which would take her away for most of the day.

'Well, you'll certainly get a good view from up there today.'

'We should do.' She looked at me. 'Are you going back to the mainland this afternoon?'

'Yes. I'll have lunch here and then push off.' I hesitated. 'Were you serious when you said you'd like sometime to see the Department's toys put through their paces?'

'I certainly was. Is it possible I could see them sometime?'

'Of course. Like all fond parents we're always glad to demonstrate our offsprings' party pieces. Shall I give you a ring in a week's time and we can arrange something?'

She agreed and gave me her address and phone number. When we rose, prior to leaving the dining-room, she said: 'It's a pity your visit has been so unsatisfactory.'

'Inconclusive, yes, but I didn't really expect it to be otherwise. It's only in books — ' I smiled '— fiction, that is — that everything has a neat, logical explanation. Anyway, when I see you in Glasgow — ' I rather liked being able to say that ' — I'll let you know if there's been any further developments.'

A quarter of an hour later I was walking up the driveway of

Carradale House. In a way I regretted accepting Leighton's invitation for in my present frame of mind I was impatient to get back to the mainland to report to Sir Mark (I was not at all anxious to report to Laura) and have done with the whole dismal business. And yet, an intruding thought pointed out, if I hadn't come here I wouldn't have met Claire. I pushed the whole matter aside and climbed the eight broad sandstone steps under the pillared portico to the glass-fronted door. Opening it, I found myself in a spacious hall. I knocked on another glass-panelled door marked 'Enquiries' and a woman's voice invited me to enter. Behind a desk a secretarial-type middle-aged woman asked if she could help.

'I'm looking for Mr. Leighton,' I replied. On learning that I was expected, she checked with someone by intercom.

'I'll take you up.' Heels clicking, she led the way across the black and white tiled floor of the hall to the foot of the white marble staircase I had noticed on my entrance. It swept up to a half-landing from which two branches curved off on either side up to the first-floor landing. The balustrade was formed of small marble pillars. It would cost a fortune to build now, I thought. In fact, it probably cost enough to build even in Victorian times. We walked along a carpeted and oak-panelled corridor with windows looking out on a cobbled courtyard. My companion knocked on a door, a voice said 'Come in' and we entered.

Leighton came out from behind a broad desk set before the wide window, hand outstretched.

'Thank you, Miss Welsh.' As I shook hands, my eye was caught by an ash-blonde young woman in a dark suit and white blouse sitting beside the desk. She stood up as Leighton introduced us and I saw that she was about thirty, with most attractive features, possessing the slightly pointed chin and heightened cheekbones so many pale blondes seem to have.

'Margaret, this is Mr. Arnott. Mr. Arnott, Miss Cornelius. Margaret looks after our female guests.'

'How do you do, Mr. Arnott?' Her voice was pleasant, her hand cool. Leighton continued in his slightly fussy manner, his hands clasped behind his back. 'I'm going to show Mr. Arnott over the house. Perhaps you'd like to join us here for coffee, Margaret, about eleven.'

'Thank you, I'd like that. I'll have coffee prepared. And I can hear what Mr.Arnott thinks of our health factory.' She smiled at me and left the room. Leighton looked after her, gave a little laugh then steered me out of the room. For some reason the meeting left me with a slight feeling of unease.

In fact the tour was quite interesting. There was a gymnasium with all the usual apparatus, in which five perspiring men, some unhappy but all determined, were being encouraged by a tough gym instructor in cream, roll-top sweater and flannels to bring some tone back to muscles almost suffocated by fat. There was a small steam bath, a heated green-tiled swimming pool in the basement, a sun-lamp room, a recreation room with a billiard table as well as other games, and a library well stocked with away-from-it-all fiction, travel, historical novels, etc. Throughout the tour, Leighton kept up an enthusiastic commentary.

'Our so-called civilisation and the pace of modern living has a lot to answer for. Frankly, I am appalled when I see the shape some of our guests arrive in. Too many business lunches, no exercise, heavy smoking (so much for the lung cancer scare!), too much social drinking, the pressure of constant decision-making —' he shrugged ' — ulcers, hypertension, overweight, insomnia, dependence upon sedatives. And yet they come here expecting us to work wonders in a fortnight. When I see them I'm glad I've always kept myself in reasonable shape.' He glanced at me. 'How old would you say I am, Arnott?'

I looked at him. I thought, fifty-fiveish, so said fifty or late forties. He sighed.

'I'm fifty-three, actually,' He smoothed his hair. 'Getting a bit thin on top but that's not important. Anyway I've heard it said that if you keep as much of your hair as I have by the time you're my age you won't lose what's left.' He thought about this for a few seconds then asked: 'How old are you, Arnott?'

'Thirty-eight.'

He sighed again. 'An ideal age. I'd give anything to be that age again with the forties ahead. Youthful insecurities and uncertainties are gone, —' are they? I thought. ' — a wealth of experience has been gathered and one's powers are at their peak.'

'I'd hate to think my powers were going in my early fifties,' I remarked mildly.

'No, no, don't get me wrong,' he said quickly. 'The fifties are good, too, but there's a definite slowing-up in performance.' He frowned and when he spoke again I wondered if it was a complete non-sequitor. 'Our women guests are in just about as bad shape as the men — too little to do, overeating, neurosis. And bitchy! At least the men try to co-operate. But the women! I pity Margaret who has to try to make them toe the line. Do you know, we caught one of them who is on a strict diet bribing one of the maids to bring in food from Brodick!'

'Isn't your treatment a bit drastic?'

'Ah, we have to be very careful. Complete medical overhaul and strict supervision — we have a resident physician — with exercises and diet, etcetera, carefully graduated to the person's condition. But that side of it is only part of the course. They go for walks, or go out fishing — remarkably soothing, that — or golfing or hill-climbing if they're fit enough.'

I supposed it could do a captain of industry a bit of good to spend a few quiet weeks unwinding here. At the same time I would have thought he'd have preferred Switzerland or the Bahamas. Though if he'd been punishing his liver too much, a secluded place near at hand like Carradale House might be a good spot in which to taper off. I wondered what scale of fees were charged. Probably as high as the ceiling, judging by the standard of equipment and the general plushiness.

'Well, let's have some coffee upstairs. You've seen it all now.' He grinned. 'Can we interest you in a stay?'

'I don't think so. I've had my exercise for the season.'

Back in his room we found Miss Cornelius setting out cups and saucers from a tray. During the idle chit-chat I wondered about Leighton and her. I thought I detected a barely perceptible air of possession about him in his attitude towards her that made me speculate on whether it was based on fact or fantasy. She on the other hand was cool and detached and, I thought, perfectly conscious of her attractiveness to the opposite sex. And not without intelligence either which didn't square with Leighton's remark on the Moor about brainy women.

A gesture of hers suddenly revealed to me the reason for my unease. She reminded me slightly of Irene. There was the same smooth, pale blonde attractiveness, perhaps the same temperament. A whole block of memories surfaced in my mind, excerpts from our three years together, the too-short courtship, the feverish, experimental, carefree honeymoon in Majorca, the growing dismay later as we discovered our disastrous incompatibility, the collision course of quarrels, the exaggerated verbal missiles launched at each other, the final shocked attempt at reconciliation, the ill-considered holiday in Arran to show her the island I'd talked so much about, the last quarrel, her furious walk-out, the car-crash, the identification, the searing self-recriminations, the attempts to forget, to hide oneself in work. I looked back over ten years and all at once was conscious of the gulf between myself and those two youngsters and how equally divided was my compassion. Something seemed to resolve itself within me and I realised that the past was finally over and done with.

I returned to the room in Carradale House, sensed that Leighton had asked a question and was waiting for an answer. I managed to re-run his words mentally and replied.

'You're quite right. I think it would be difficult for a Martian visiting this planet to believe we're rational. Bombers and missiles in a state of constant readiness, manned by men with no conceivable quarrel with each other, kindly, essentially moral, yet prepared to fry and torture each others' women and children in their millions if ordered to do so.'

Leighton smiled. 'The big stick, the deterrent. Don't you sometimes wish you could turn the clock back, Arnott?'

'No, I don't think so. I prefer to live now. I don't know what the future will bring but I do know that if mankind is at its most crucial epoch — and I certainly believe it is — I want to be around to see what happens.'

'Personally,' said Miss Cornelius, 'I think our only hope is that the women take over. We couldn't make a bigger mess of things than you men have.'

'God forbid.' Leighton's face sketched horror. 'I'm not yet convinced you should have been given the vote.'

Miss Cornelius laughed. 'Kinde, Kuche, Kirche, that's Kenneth.' She gazed at me inquiringly. 'By the way, Mr. Arnott, what branch of science do you work in?'

I told them. In fact, now that I had the opening, I told them why I had come to the island, on the outside chance that they could contribute something of value. They listened attentively, just as everyone else did, I thought bitterly. Leighton turned to the woman.

'We remember the incident well, don't we? Of course in an island of this size, anything out of the ordinary soon gets around. Postmen, drivers of grocers' vans, and so on, they all form a communications network — a sort of latter day bush telegraph. But in point of fact it was Fullerton who told me. I was over at the Tormore Hotel the evening of the day they found him. We often have a chinwag, you know, talking over old times; we were both in the last little unpleasantness. Bert was one of the Few who survived; I spent three years with Monty.' He shook his head. 'I must say, hearing about your friend gave me a bit of a shock. It must have been him I saw the previous day up at the Circles. I had taken Bran up after lunch to give him some exercise and I noticed this bloke measuring and probing. I thought he was someone from the Ministry of Works. They took over the site a number of years ago.'

'Did you speak to him?'

'Passed the time of day with him. Asked him what he was doing.' He hesitated, looked carefully at me, then went on. 'I hope you don't mind my saying so, but he was a bit short with me. Almost cagey, if you know what I mean. As if he had a lot of things on his mind, didn't like the intrusion. Anyway, I left him to it.' He stroked the short goatee beard as if wanting to say more but Miss Cornelius butted in.

'Have you had any luck in your enquiries, Mr. Arnott?'

I described what I'd done. They sympathised with me on the negative outcome, the conversation veered to an account of a climbing accident on A'Chir Ridge two years back, and ten minutes later I took my leave of them.

After lunch I settled my bill with Mr. Fullerton, packed the few things I had brought and left the Tormore Hotel. The sunshine struck a million reflections from the waters of the Kilbrannan Sound as I turned the car inland on to the Machrie Road. On the winding route over the Moor I looked once to my right across the rolling bracken and heather-covered moss to where the stones stood then stared ahead again to Glen Eisbeg and the String Road. When I came down to the eastern side of the island and drove along to the pier I found I had an hour to wait. I parked the car on the seafront and sat behind the wheel, gazing out over the bay and thinking moodily about my complete failure as a detective.

You'd better stick to cybernetics after this, I told myself. When I let myself into the flat in Hillhead Street it was seven p.m. Picking up the three envelopes and the copy of the *Glasgow Herald* lying on the floor under the letterbox, I entered the kitchen and switched on the kettle. My mail consisted of an electricity bill, an exhortation to buy a new encyclopaedia, and a lecture request from the Young Conservative Association. By the time I'd unpacked and had a meal of sorts it was seven forty-five. I found I hadn't the heart to phone Laura that evening — I felt it better to see her and it would be too late to visit her that night in any case. In fact I went to bed about ten and in the fifteen minutes I lay in the dark before sleep came, the events of the past forty-eight hours re-ran themselves through the projector of my mind. Just before consciousness dissolved, I seemed to be picking up the *Glasgow Herald* and my mail and remarking to no one in particular that mail left on the hall table was much more significant. Feeling that I was within grasp of some truth, if only I could interpret my subconscious's remark, I fell asleep.

In the Department next morning I informed Sir Mark of the entirely negative outcome of my visit. He listened quietly while I gave him the gist of my conversations with Fullerton and his wife, Claire Stewart and the sergeant and described the search he and I had made on the Doon and at the foot of the cliff.

'I'm sorry, sir. I seem to have drawn a complete blank.'

He smiled momentarily. 'Well, it was an outside chance at best. The only thing is, will it convince Laura that there's nothing more to be done?' He looked at me, his sharp blue eyes belying the vague halo of spunsilk hair. 'You'd better see her.'

I hesitated. 'What's your opinion now, sir?'

'About his death?'

'Yes. And the work he was supposed to be doing.'

The Old Man was silent for a full five seconds. Then he sighed and shook his head. 'I haven't got one. If anything, I have a leaning towards the simple accident theory.'

'But his workpapers?'

'I know. Whatever it was, I'm beginning to think he destroyed it.' He rubbed his head in exasperation. 'Roger, I don't suppose we'll ever know the truth about John's death. To my mind, the most sensible course of action we can take now is to close the file and simply remember him as we knew him — a first-rate scientist and a good man.'

'Death closes all . . . . !' I thought. I nodded and turned to go. I had the door open when he said: 'Roger, if you've nothing terribly urgent to do, why not try to see Laura this afternoon?'

'I'll do that,' I promised.

Upstairs in my room I dialled the number and waited, listening to the burr-burr tone. There was no reply. With a craven sense of relief I hung up and began work after asking Anne to call the number at hourly intervals throughout the day. About four p.m. I got through. As I expected, she asked me over that evening. I gave her a detailed account of my visit to the island though I was careful to edit out the sergeant's speculations. She did not interrupt once.

'So that's the situation, Laura,' I concluded. 'I really do not see that there's anything more anyone can do. And I'm terribly sorry I do not seem to have done anything at all to help you.'

She sat still, facing me, her hands in her lap, a bewildered, yet resigned look on her face. 'You have helped, Roger. I'm still totally unconvinced Johnny's death was an accident but I agree with you — there doesn't seem to be anything to do. Perhaps as time goes on and I can look at it from a more detached viewpoint it'll make more sense.'

I doubted it but said nothing to disagree.

'What are your immediate plans?'

'I don't know. Probably I'll shut up the house and go down to Mother's for a bit. She's not too fit yet.'

Privately I hoped she'd return quite soon to the work she'd been doing before she met Johnny and that ultimately she'd marry again. You should talk, I told myself. Soon after, I left. She thanked me again and I drove back to Glasgow feeling thoroughly depressed.

Ten days came and went. Once more I became caught up in research and development concerning Project Rover, trying to accomplish as much as possible before the Martinmas term with its lecturing and tutorial load cut large slices out of the week. Correcting the September examination scripts took up two days. Most evenings I worked, going back to the Department after having high tea in the College Club. The inevitable recession in my memory of the events surrounding Johnny's death took place except when I had leisure to think or when we suddenly realised the gap he had left in our research team. I thought the whole thing over again, for example, in the club one day after lunch when I noticed the University's advert in the current *Nature* for someone to take his place. But I found to my dismay that strongly colouring these thoughts was the knowledge that Claire would be home next day.

On one of the evenings, I had dinner with Clark Desmond. I had done some work for him on his TV science news programme in the past, mainly talks or question-and-answer snippets on current developments in the cybernetic field. He was an engaging young chap, in appearance reminiscent of Harold Lloyd, with a remarkably efficient memory that soaked up all experience. After a spell in the wilderness as an angry young man with CND sympathies, he had become accepted as one of the best science commentators in the medium. This time he wanted me to discuss a report that an electronic computer in London had written two songs that had made the Top Twenty. After commenting that I had been under the impression that they were all written by computers, I promised to turn up the following evening at the studio and say my piece. When I did, I found the usual scene of apparent chaos on the floor with cameras, boom-mikes, lights and technicians everywhere with a pop group being rehearsed. All four members, who in saner times would have qualified as suitable cases for treatment, were miming with loose-jointed and blatantly-suggestive gymnastic fervour to their latest disc, which happened to be one of the computer hits. In the dimly-lit monitor room, Desmond grinned at me. 'It's godawful, isn't it?' Swinging back to the mike, he flipped over a switch. 'That's terrific, boys, just terrific.' He caught my eye and had the grace to look sheepish.

The television world, especially commercial TV, has always fascinated me in its complete contrast to the academic world I work in. The respective scales of values have little or no common ground, the working rules are entirely different. I would certainly think twice of phoning a lab in California to obtain urgently required data I knew they had: I have seen Clark Desmond spend half an hour on the transatlantic phone trying to track down some potentially newsworthy report. If it was true that a TV licence was a licence to print money, it was equally true that they knew how to spend it.

Between final rehearsals and programme time he told me that after working for years on a shoestring budget (my eyebrows went up) he had finally converted the top brass to the realisation that science and technology are here to say.

'Oh yes,' he said, 'you'd be surprised how many scientific illiterates there still are at the top. But even they have discovered that this is the space era, the era of spare-part surgery, the cracking of the genetic code, the lot. Science is news, they tell me. It influences our everyday lives, its new developments raise tremendously important ethical and moral issues. It's all happening! And so they've opened the cornucopia for me. In fact they intend to send out the first of the spare-no-expense series of 'Man in the Scientific Age' via Syncom satellite to damn near everywhere in the world. You know: see what the boys in the U.K. can do.'

I congratulated him, got the date and time from him and promised to look in.

Unaware that events were fast catching up with me, I gave Claire a day to settle in then phoned. She seemed pleased to hear from me and agreed to have dinner with me in the Club prior to coming back to the Department. On the date we chose I picked her up about six-fifteen from her flat in Westbank Quadrant. The flat was on the third floor and I pressed the bell-push, trying to convince myself that my quickened breathing was entirely due to having walked too briskly up three flights of stairs. My sense of excitement when she opened the door and welcomed me laughed at my attempts at self-deception.

Over dinner we renewed and developed our acquaintance then drove down to the Department. There were some lights on in a number of windows as usual, where some of the staff were working late. Burroughs, the night-janitor, poked his head out of his office like an old turtle from its shell to check on us then retired to continue reading his *Evening Citizen*. I gave Claire a slightly extended version of the tour we keep for visiting politicians and other non-scientific types. She was charmed with Dozey, who still survived in spite of our decision to dismantle him. He followed us about faithfully while I showed Claire the repertoire of tricks the other automata possessed. Some were versions of the standard Grey Walter tortoises, others were entirely our own design. I explained what we were trying to learn from these constructions before introducing her to EDITH (Electronic Device Imitating Thought), our educated computer. With an effort I kept my face straight as I watched the expression of bemused incredulity develop on Claire's face.

'Edith, I've brought someone to see you.'

'Hullo.' The soft chiming tones brought Claire's eyes round to me. I nodded in encouragement. She hesitated but took the plunge.

'Hullo Edith.'

'I have not met you before, have I?'

'N-no.'

'Are you a friend of Dr. Arnott's?'

'Yes.' She gasped. 'How does she — ?'

'She doesn't recognise your voice. That is, the frequency analysis she did on it doesn't match any stored in her memory. But if you ever speak to her again she will remember you and everything said on this occasion. Won't you, Edith?'

'Yes, Dr. Arnott. Have you any problems?'

Have I any problems! Oh yes, indeed, Edith, but not the sort you can handle. I let the two girls chat for a few minutes before switching off the computer. As we walked away Claire looked at me with something like horror in her eyes.

'It seems alive.'

'I know. You find yourself respecting her feelings and being polite. In fact, people have sworn after talking to Edith that she understands them better than their psychiatrist. But don't let her fool you. There's no personality or consciousness there, just a vast memory packed with data, some logical circuits, association networks, correlation devices and input and output channels.' I wondered if Claire was convinced or if she felt, as many people did, that 'They' were taking over. We finished the tour and I switched out the laboratory lights.

'Well, that's that. You've seen it all. You will now go away with a lasting impression that we spend our days building toys and playing with them.'

'Well, don't you?' She smiled. We left the building, said goodnight to Burroughs and I drove her back to Westbank Quadrant. When she asked me up for some coffee, I accepted.

She showed me into the lounge, switched on the radiator, and told me to sit down while she got coffee ready. Left alone in the room I examined it with interest. It was bright and modern yet comfortable with different papers on each wall that contrasted without clashing. The alcoves on either side of the fireplace held bookshelves heavy with multi-coloured hard-covers and paperbacks. Under the tall, curtained windows that overlooked the River Kelvin stood a sofa. There was no sign of any work-area, no writing desk or tape recorder or typewriter, and I supposed she had turned one of the other rooms into a study. When she returned with a tray bearing cups and saucers, sugar bowl, etc. I was looking over the titles of the books on the shelves. Her taste was catholic — travel, biography, fiction, the classics, quite a lot of poetry, books in French and German and, I saw with interest, she still had some of her schoolbooks. I lifted one — a Hall and Knight's *Higher Algebra* — opened it and saw written in ink on the fly-leaf 'Claire Nicola Stewart, Old Hall, Painters Green, Sussex, England, the Earth, the Solar System, the Galaxy, the Universe (turn right at the first galaxy past Andromeda).'

I caught myself smiling: it seemed so long ago that I had done the same sort of thing myself. Under the address she had written Form V and the date and I thought back to what I had been doing when she was engaged with the intricacies of the binomial theorem. I became even more conscious of our age difference. And yet . . . .

I left an hour later. She had agreed to have dinner with me again and to let me take her to the first of the Scottish Orchestra concerts of the new season. When I reached Hillhead Street I felt alert and a little drunk and very conscious that it was possible my life was entering a new and fabulously different phase.

Five more days passed. On the early afternoon of the fifth day I was walking down from the College Club towards the Department after lunch when our day-janitor hailed me. He was carrying the afternoon mail, collected from the central office.

'Only one for you, Dr. Arnott.'

I took the long airmail envelope from him and looked at it. It was from Don Shapiro, whom I had wanted to see in the States but failed to because he was off on holiday at Cape Cod. Once in my room, I sat down behind the desk and slit open the red and blue edged envelope. There were two enclosures — a typed letter from Shapiro and an ordinary closed envelope with British postage stamps on it. The inner envelope was addressed to me, care of Professor Don Shapiro, in handwriting that caused me to suck my breath in sharply. I put it down slowly and read the communication from Shapiro.

'Dear Dr. Arnott,

I was really sorry to miss you on your recent visit to the States, but Joe Leinster and Peter Fulton filled me in on the talks you had with them. I sure hope the rest of your stay was enjoyable and profitable and that I will see you at the next I.C.U. meeting in Paris.

'And now I have an apology to make to you. Before going off on vacation, I told my secretary not to forward any mail and very unfortunately this letter to you somehow got in among the heap of mail on my desk awaiting my return. It should of course have been handed to you when you passed through here but never was. I do hope that the delay has not caused any trouble.

'With all best wishes,
'Very sincerely yours,

'Don Shapiro.'

73

I laid the flimsy sheet aside and stared at the other letter, the letter from Johnny that I should have received four weeks previously.

5   Cry from a Dead Sorcerer

I picked up the letter, noticing with a heightening of my tension that it was postmarked 'Machrie'. With more care than usual I used the paperknife on my desk to slit open the envelope and drew out four sheets of paper. Unfolding them I saw that they were covered on both sides with Johnny's handwriting. I began to read.

Tormore Hotel,
Machrie,
Isle of Arran

'*Dear Roger,*

I'm sorry to butt in on your American tour like this, especially since there is a chance that I am panicking unnecessarily but I feel that the reasons I give below will be adequate.

'*You may remember that on one memorable occasion when you visited us, the conversation turned to the subject of discoveries that should not be made or inventions that should not be invented. After such flippant ones as "Wad some power the giftie gie us to see oursel's as others see us", we finally agreed that one serious possibility received full marks. As we discussed the implications our opinion hardened and we came to the conclusion that if ever there was a "man was not meant to meddle in such matters" case this was it.*

'*Well, Roger, I am afraid I have meddled in such matters and now, like the sorcerer's apprentice, I wish I hadn't. When I think back now on how I went in deeper and deeper, like a drug addict getting hooked, I am appalled. At the same time, I think that as a scientist with more than your fair share of curiosity, you will understand the temptation.*

'*Anyway, I did it! Even now I feel almost sick with excitement when I recall my first uses of it.*

'*If I'd had sufficient strength of mind, I suppose I'd have destroyed it and burned my notes there and then but I didn't. I kept hoping that I'd see a way out of giving it all up. How many men have said that through the ages, I wonder? But, as you well know, the advantages of possessing this are incalculable. On the other hand, the disadvantages — My God!*

'*Just after I'd completed my task, Laura's mother took ill and she went down to England to nurse her. I seized the opportunity to come to Arran to have a few days' rest — I'd been going non-stop at it for weeks, ever since it first dawned on me that it was a possibility. In any case, I wanted to potter about among the Circles again and think, well away from anyone, think very carefully as to what I should do.*

'*Frankly, I still hadn't made up my mind when I first noticed I was being followed, wherever I went. Believe me, Roger, I kid you not, as the saying goes. Sometimes one man kept me in sight, sometimes another. I took some convincing, I can tell you, for by this time the mental turmoil I was in was really something and I honestly wondered at first if my mind was going and I was imagining things. However I thought I'd better take some precautions.*

'*It became clear to me that something was really up when I returned from dinner this evening to my room and found that it and my things had been searched. I therefore have to assume that in some way others have discovered that I have been successful and are after my discovery. How they have found out I have no idea. No! That's a lie. There is one possibility that is terrifying me and which I must give to you. Perhaps I am not the first one. You will see what I mean if you think about it. I am not sold on this idea myself but if it is true then what I am trying to do with this letter is pointless. Yet I have to take the chance and I have to lumber you with my troubles, because in one way it is the only precaution I can take and in another, I honestly think you possess all the factors in your makeup to come to the best possible decision.*

'*The searchers did not get anything for there was nothing to get by that time. I had, praise be, already buried everything. Again, you and you only will understand when I say that the slaughter stone marks the spot. It may be that your decision will be to leave it undisturbed. Okay. That will be all right by me. Whatever you do I accept.*

'You may think I'm being needlessly melodramatic. I hope to God I am, but you know perfectly well that in this crazy world of ours there are lots of lovely people who would think a Belsen a very small price to pay for this.

'I shall give this letter to the boot-boy to post. And then I think I shall pack up and get back home. I hope I am completely wrong about all this and that we'll have a good laugh over my fears when I see you again.

'With all best wishes and my sincere apologies for loading this on to you,

'Yours,

Johnny.'

Quite slowly I put down the sheets of paper, a cold, dead feeling congealing my action. The familiar room (University Grants Committee standard size) with its neat shelves of sober textbooks, lecture notes and data files, formed an unobtrusive and incongruous background to the turbulent, leapfrogging thoughts that raced through my head. So many things were spotlight clear now — or made a lot more sense than before. Above all I knew with a sick excitement that dried my mouth what Johnny had created. I recalled very clearly the occasion when he and Laura and I had sat in their sitting-room at Boquhan in front of the log fire and talked and gradually acknowledged the staggering implications bound up in it. But it had been idle speculation then, a charming topic of conversation. Why couldn't you leave it there, Johnny? I thought. Now it's killed you and now I've got to pick up the pieces and whatever your faith in me I'm not at all sure I'm the right man to do it. The slaughter stone. I knew about that too.

When I picked up the letter and re-read it, my hands trembled and I felt the itchy trickle of sweat in my brows. Yet a feeling of admiration came over me at the ingenuity Johnny had shown in devising, on the spur of the moment and under pressure, the means of getting out word to me, letting me know exactly what he had done and where to look, without giving anything away if the letter had gone astray. And yet — I found a salt taste in my mouth as I licked my lips — he was dead and quite suddenly I recalled the confused thought I'd had about my mail the night I'd arrived home from Brodick. "Mail left on the hall table is much more significant." A clear-cut picture arose in my mind of me removing the letters from the hall table the day I came back from the

States. The flat had been shut up for weeks, it was musty-smelling, yet the mail was lying on the hall table. Someone had been in the flat in my absence. Someone had picked up the letters and magazines from behind the door and forgotten to replace them. If they had searched the flat — for this letter I held in my hand? — they had been more careful for I had discovered nothing out of place. Or perhaps it was only the mail they had been after. Quite possibly it had been removed, examined and returned, a process that probably was still going on. And if it hadn't been for this letter being handed straight to me by the janitor, it might never have reached me.

My thoughts leaped on. Johnny's death was still a mystery. There was still a possibility that he had committed suicide to prevent his knowledge getting into the wrong hands but I wasn't sold on that one. Otherwise how had they known to follow me and monitor my mail? And that thought led to another frightening possibility, namely that they had killed Johnny after getting all they wanted from him. If that was so the slaughter stone would cover nothing and I — I found myself rubbing my jaw, my gaze fixed on the door as if I expected it to open deliberately and reveal. . . But they had waited until now for this letter. If they knew I had received it. But they didn't. I stood up, pushed the letter into my inside pocket and went to the door. In the corridor, my nervous glances up and down made me tongue lash myself into an attempt at normal behaviour. Once down the stairs I entered Anne's office. She ceased typing and looked up. I crossed to the timetable shelf.

'When will Sir Mark be back?' I asked, my fingers flicking over the pages of the British Railways booklet.

'He said he'd be in late this afternoon. He's flying back this morning.' She paused. 'Can I help you?'

'No, thanks. Look, Anne, something important has come up that I must attend to. If anyone inquires for me say I'll be away the rest of the day and possibly tomorrow too'. I saw that with a bit of luck I could catch the *Glen Sannox* sailing at 6.10 p.m. and be in Arran an hour later. I slipped the timetable into its place beside the BEA, BOAC and other brochures and turned to find Anne looking at me, a curious, almost watchful, expression on her face.

'Nothing wrong, Dr. Arnott?'

'No, not at all. Why?'

She hesitated. 'I'm sorry. You looked . . . well . . . a bit harassed.'

To put it mildly.

'We live in a harassing age, Anne. See you later.'

I hope. I left the office and the building. Two minutes later I was on the road to Fairlie, the off-season sailing point for the car ferry. Twice I stopped, once at an ironmonger's shop to buy a spade and a torch which went into the back seat, the second time at a small garage on a long straight stretch of road. While the attendant operated the pump I got out of the car and looked back along the way I had come. No one seemed to be following me. My spirits heightened somewhat, I paid the man and waited for change, my eyes on the poster depicting the cowboy-suited sultry wench standing legs apart, petrol nozzle at the ready.

'Ride Regent, the lively one.'

I grinned involuntarily, recalling Johnny's dry comment on one occasion I'd been in his car: "What a strange name to give anyone."

I received my change and started off again. Fairlie Pier was reached without incident and when I drove the car up the ramp on to the *Glen Sannox* I felt sure I was on my own.

There were only seven other cars in the car-deck. My first intention of sitting in the Armstrong-Siddeley during the fifty-five minute journey and thinking rationally lasted me five minutes only before I shied away mentally from the confused directions my mind was taking. In any event, I told myself, I couldn't make any plans until later. Leaving the car, I climbed the steps to the lower lounge and toured the ship, moving restlessly from one part to the next, scanning the faces of the passengers in an effort to detect anything deceitful or menacing about them. There were few people on board and all seemed innocent and reasonably carefree. Regardless of their fate the little rascals played. . . . I gripped the teak rail, my eyes and ears inattentive to the raucous importunities of the wheeling seagulls. The sky was dull and there was a nasty wind coming up the Firth, whipping the waves to white patches atop the rolling green swells. The Indian summer weather was getting a bit tattered from overuse. I went back to the lounge.

On one of the turquoise-blue upholstered seats I found a *Daily Express*, crossword completed. I glanced through it. The Prime Minister denied once again that phone-tapping was in common use by security forces throughout Great Britain. There was a heartening visit to a Regional Civil Defence headquarters where the walls of the underground network of rooms had been painted in pastel greens, yellows, blues and pinks, colours chosen by a team of psychologists to soothe the nerves of people who might be cooped up in there for days. 'Although half the country's population may well be killed, at least twenty-five to thirty millions would be left to be helped by us.' said a spokesman. I tried to visualise five million small children and couldn't.

I turned the page and learned that fashion was again in the Italian style, with Haute Couture clothes deliciously versatile, with space-age glitter-mesh, arrow-narrow pants and two-tone bodices (for the men) and cylindrical evening dresses slit thigh-high to reveal polka-dot stockings (for the women). On another page, James Bond — every-man's fantasy figure — was making love to another woman and after an Old Firm game, twenty-five arrests for drunken and disorderly behaviour had been made. The magistrate said that such bestial conduct would be dealt with severely in future and fined them five pounds each.

A surge of relief swept through me as I looked out and saw the Brodick shore approach. Downstairs and in the car once more I listened to the sounds of the ferry docking at the pier. The second carload on the lift included the Siddeley and once beyond the pierhead I turned to the left up the steep one-in-eight hill towards Lamlash. Every so often I glanced into the rear mirror but there was no sign of a follower. Although I grudged every minute I spent in this way, I had no intention of doing what I had come to do in broad daylight which was why I was taking the long way round. I noted with satisfaction that the weather was deteriorating further, a rain-mist causing me to switch on the wipers as I passed through Lamlash and crossed the bridge beside the High School. My eyes caught the 'police' sign above the front door of the sergeant's cottage and I thought of Johnny's letter and knew I couldn't stop.

At the road junction I veered the car on to the narrow, twisting Ross Road. Like the String, it crosses the island, snaking upwards to a height of almost a thousand feet between the desolate moors before descending to the coast near Slidderywater Foot. Down there I turned north and quite leisurely completed the rest of my South Arran tour. When I arrived at the farm gate at the beginning of the track leading up to the Tormore Circles, it was eight-ten and a thin drizzle from low clouds was watering down the evening light. With care I steered the Siddeley along the rutted farm road, stopping twice more to lift open and shut behind me dilapidated gates that impeded progress. The rough granite shapes of Fingal's Cauldron Stones appeared as I reached the final rise and I drove the last two hundred yards along the track before stopping.

Once out of the car, I spent half a minute scrutinising the silent moors and hills. There wasn't a living creature to be seen. Mist screened the hills to the south-east of Blackwaterfoot but fortunately the drizzle had passed on towards Glen Eisbeg. I retrieved the torch and spade from the back seat and began to tramp down past the ruined walls of the nearer cottage towards the circle marked by the massive single sandstone survivor. The shower of rain hadn't saturated the peat to any appreciable extent after the long, dry summer but the myriad beads of moisture on the vegetation stems soon soaked the foot of my trousers.

At the circle I quickly found what I was looking for, a sandstone slab lying half-buried in the peat with six deep parallel grooves weathered in its upper face. The slaughter stone. I remembered Johnny pointing it out to me on his scale drawing of that circle. 'There is a marvellous local legend that the grooves were cut to carry away the blood. Real Hammer Film stuff.'

I stuck the spade in the ground and examined the rough tufts of vegetation in the immediate area of the stone edge. The surface could have been disturbed but with cattle and sheep chewing and churning up the moss it was by no means certain. I glanced around the darkening horizon again, feeling unpleasantly conspicuous, then began digging. I used the edge of the spade to chop through the tough heather roots in areas a foot square before spading them out. As I lifted the dark brown peat-blocks I felt my heart pound and my stomach tighten for it was now obvious that the vegetation had been cut up quite recently. I continued to dig, excavating greasy lumps, the spade rapidly becoming clogged. Soon I had worked my way right round the stone without success. The slab was now completely bare. I dropped the spade, realising for the first time that my face burned like a furnace and my breath gasped through my open mouth. Wiping away the trickles of sweat on my forehead, I examined the sandstone. It was obviously a fragment of a fallen pillar and did not seem to be beyond my strength to shift.

When I stuck the edge of the spade under it and levered, it moved. I gripped the rough underside of its edge and strained upwards. It came up, certainly too easily if it had lain there for centuries or millenia, and I toppled it over. I dug out the area it had covered but found nothing. By now dusk had reduced visibility to the point where I had to peer closely at the work area but there was no doubt in my mind. The ground had been dug up before. And that meant. . . . I straightened up, instantaneously and icily conscious that I was no longer alone on the Moor.

Three figures, spread through one hundred and eighty degrees, were converging on me. They must have approached through the gloom while I heaved at the sandstone. I gripped the spade, fear and indecision freezing me to the spot, my head turning from one to the other in a futile effort to keep all three in view simultaneously. The centre figure spoke.

'Well, Dr. Arnott, any success?'

6 The Sheep and the Goats

I said nothing. Leighton stopped six feet from me. The others moved a little past me so that I lost any chance of running. Indeed in my state of confusion, in my immediate attempt to revalue the situation, I did not know what I wanted to do. Leighton stuffed his hands in the pocket of the heavy tweed coat he wore and peered at my excavations.

'I don't think the Ministry would like this.' He kicked aside a thick peat. 'Perhaps we'd better help Dr. Arnott to replace the turf.' He indicated the man on his left with a nod. 'If you give Tilney the spade, he and Davis will tidy things up. Go on, there's a good chap. You've had a worrying journey for nothing and I think you're entitled to some explanations.'

I found myself handing over the spade. Explanations I needed. I now had no intention of bounding off over the heather like a startled rabbit. The two men — whose names I forgot immediately and henceforth, for some reason best known to my subconcious, labelled Cain and Abel — set to work, Cain shovelling the earth and peat back into the hole after they had replaced the slab in its original position, Abel putting together the jigsaw pieces of turf I had chopped out. Meanwhile Leighton stood beside me, a ghost of a smile just visible, his eyes flicking at times from my face to the repair work. Through my mind a mixture of thoughts danced, producing as wide a variety of emotions. They had known I was coming. Or I'd been followed after all. Had they emptied the cache? If so, why bother to wait for me? Ah yes, the letter; how did they know I had it? If they were responsible for Johnny's death then I wasn't in the best of places. Leighton's eyes regarded me with amusement. He knows most of what's running through my head, I told myself bitterly.

The two men straightened up. Cain used a tuft of heather to wipe off the spade.

Leighton smiled. 'Now, Dr. Arnott, we'll go back to Carradale House for some supper. You must be feeling like something to eat. Anyway, it'll be more comfortable to talk there than here on this decidedly draughty moor.'

He acknowledged my non-committal 'All right' with an enthusiastic 'Good!' and we began to trudge back across the uneven ground, Leighton beside me, Cain and Abel close behind. As we climbed the slope beside the ruined farmhouse an engine fired and a Land Rover bumped round the corner. The driver gunned the motor and the vehicle roared past us up on to the cart-track beyond the parked Siddeley. So now I knew where they had been waiting.

'You won't mind giving us a lift back,' said Leighton, 'and then on the way I can fill you in a bit.'

As I followed the Land Rover's red tail lights along the rutted peatroad, with my two passengers in the back, I appreciated how neatly I had been boxed in. As I anticipated, he said very little of relevance during the journey to Carradale House. Indeed, apart from admitting that he had been 'less than frank' during my previous visit, and assuring me more than once that he would in due course explain everything to me, he contented himself with a few neutral conversational comments.

Once in the spacious hall of Carradale House ('we'll put the car in the garage for you — plenty of room') I was shown into a bathroom to wash up. I closed the white-painted door, crossed to the washhand basin and began running in hot water. My hands were filthy, the nails Indian-ink black. I peered at my reflection in the mirror and saw that where I had removed sweat from my forehead I had added streaky brown-black peat-stains. I scrubbed my hands, dried them, removed my jacket and tie and washed my face. The ritual and the warm towels from the heated towel rack restored my morale a little. Straightening my tie, I combed my hair, then halted, comb six inches from my head as the thought hit me that Johnny may have gazed at his reflection in this same mirror. I opened the bathroom door and re-entered the bright hall. From a polished oak settle just inside the hall, Cain (or was it Abel?) got up.

'Please come with me, sir.'

I climbed the deep-carpeted stairs to the second floor with him, walked along the corridor to the far end where Leighton's rooms were located and waited while he knocked at the door. A voice said 'Come!' (it would, I thought), my companion opened the door and I entered. The door closed behind me. I had time to notice there was a roaring log fire in the wide Dutch-tiled fireplace before my attention was held by Miss Cornelius coming forward to meet me, hand outstretched, casque of fair hair reflecting the light from the ceiling fixture.

'Dr. Arnott, how nice to see you again. Please come through to the dining-room. It's only a buffet supper, I'm afraid.'

I shook hands with her, nodded, and as I released her cool slim fingers I wondered what in hell's name the etiquette books recommended for such occasions. In the panelled dining-room, the table had been set for three (no tablecloth, but individual fawn-coloured mats on the dark polished surface, gleaming cutlery positioned about them). Over by the large sideboard, Leighton was fussing now over the dishes it carried.

'Ah, Arnott, come and help yourself. There's soup over there, meats in the middle and greens, etcetera at that end. I've also a bottle of Nuits St. Georges 1962 that's coming up nicely to room temperature.'

Like one of the Department's automata I selected what I wanted from the heated dishes and returned to the table to take the seat indicated. Miss Cornelius sat down opposite me. Leighton helped himself then poured the wine before taking his place at the head of the table on my right. I surprised myself by being both hungry and thirsty and dismissed the confused thought of the possibility of the food and drink being drugged as a highly impractical one. At the same time though, I resolved to refuse anything that seemed to be being forced on me in the conjuror's sense and then, at this point in my far from clear thoughts, it came to me again how thoroughly unsuited I was for all this. I accepted a dinner-roll from the basket Miss Cornelius offered and a part of me sniggered mentally when I hesitated and felt easier when both she and Leighton also took rolls and butter.

I noticed, too, as the meal progressed, that the combination of strain during the past few hours, the work on the cold open moor and its purpose, the heat of the log-fire and the excellent supper before me was relaxing me, producing an almost dream-like feeling of dissociation from the unfolding situation. Watch it, I admonished myself.

'I think the best way I can begin,' said Leighton, 'is to remind you of our last meeting here.' He placed his empty soup-plate on the sideboard and began to choose items from the dishes. 'We talked about the impossibility of deciding between the "disaster" or "ever onward and upward" views of the near future of mankind.' He cocked his head over his shoulder in enquiry as I remained silent. 'Come now, Arran, we're not going to make much progress if you're not going to be

84

sociable.' Out of the corner of my eye I caught Miss Cornelius, looking like a TV commercial for gracious living, watching me steadily, as if with amusement.

'I remember.'

'Good!' He talked like a tutor dragging discussion from a particularly unresponsive extra-mural class. 'Now the fact that we cannot decide shows how dangerously unstable the social evolution of man is. And how easily manipulatory it is.' He returned to his seat. 'Let me refill your glass.' He likes the sound of his own voice, I thought. Leighton replaced the bottle in its cradle and went on.

'This situation is new but new only to a vastly enhanced degree. It was recognised some sixty years ago by a small group of influential men in Edwardian England. They also saw how modern communications, the power of the press, science and engineering were shrinking the world, enclosing it in a network so that by pulling and manipulating some nodes, all parts could be influenced.'

My mind seemed to have seized up completely, except that some hazy assessment of the possible relevance of his words to the present situation began to nudge at the threshold.

'The First World War shook this group's belief in the rationality of mankind. Men were fools and idiots and died miserably by their millions in filthy mud, sheep brain-washed into their deaths by goats. And after the conflict, the victors, in their fear and shortsighted incompetence, viciously ground down the vanquished, laying the foundations of a bigger war twenty years on.'

Leighton drank a little, a ruby spark reflected from his glass as he set it down. 'And so the group decided to initiate a take-over bid, to use modern parlance, the operation to be conducted on a very long-term basis. It began a process of recruitment, entrenchment and manipulation, all conducted in complete secrecy. The acronym chosen was ISGAR — International Society for Guidance and Rule.'

Leighton smiled at the expression on my face. 'The group grew in number, became truly international. It instituted sub-groups and various levels in the hierarchy. Most of the members indeed have no idea for whom they are working. For example, by the very nature of intelligence work, it is possible to recruit people as agents to work happily and faithfully for ISGAR, under the firm conviction that they are serving Britain's security forces. Again, you would be surprised if you knew the percentage of the take from organised vice in the States that goes ultimately into ISGAR's account. You see, Arnott, long ago we decided that in this idiotic and messy world, we would be fools not to use any means whatsoever of hastening the day when we can choose what pages of history to write. So, to get to the point when we run things and not run the ever-present risk of the Yahoos destroying us, we deceive, suborn, bribe, blackmail, assassinate — yes, even a President, if necessary. You name it; we do it.' He turned his head. 'Margaret, would you like to pour coffee?'

I watched Miss Cornelius bring across the coffee-percolator, answered her bright query as to how I took mine, watched her fill my cup, spooned brown sugar into it, then stared at Leighton again. He seemed serious.

'But the Second War —,' I began.

'That was what showed ISGAR that the problem of effective control was orders of magnitude more difficult than previously believed. It was the problem of the cone balanced on its apex, easy to start toppling but difficult to control once in motion. In our blue-print we wanted the dictators to rule Europe but not by war. We helped to build them and tried to keep England and France quiet as long as possible but the event showed us how far we still had to go in creative effective control networks. War *was* declared and after that we had to go underground in earnest until six years later. Since the last war ended we have been rebuilding on a much vaster scale. Industrial espionage, infiltration into government circles and military installations, even into university research laboratories where discoveries may be made that would be of interest to us, television and other mass media. Every important and influential walk of life.'

I had a sudden vision of a silver-grey nervous system spreading like a cancer throughout a body, grasping and taking over each vital organ.

Leighton's confident, precise tones continued. 'To understate the situation, we have certainly surpassed the state we were in in 1939. But even yet, even yet, we still require one thing more. When we get it . . .' his head nodded slowly '. . . . then . . .' He seemed to see images that we didn't, images that held him spellbound.

I finished my coffee. Suppose it were all true. Suppose Leighton's assessment of ISGAR's ability was accurate. I looked from one to the other and then asked the obvious question.

'Why tell me all this?'

Leighton rose. 'Shall we go through to the sitting-room?' We followed him. Still acting the part of the gracious host, he offered brandy or a liqueur. I refused. He waved me into a large armchair beside the fire. Miss Cornelius, all softness and smoothness, curled up in another armchair opposite me. Leighton availed himself of the psychological advantage of standing.

'You have given us a great deal of trouble, Dr. Arnott — quite inadvertently, I hasten to add. All because of this letter Dr. Marshall wrote you.' I felt my head move. 'Oh yes. We know about it. Dr. Marshall's discovery —never mind how we found out — seemed of such importance that we had to get it. Being in charge of the local group — Carradale House and its legitimate activities make an excellent cover — I was detailed to collect it when it was learned that Marshall was coming down here. We tried first of all to obtain what we wanted by searching his room. This being unproductive, we had to remove him.'

I felt a pulse throb in my head and my jaw-muscles tightened. I concentrated more closely on the measured statements coming from his prissy little mouth.

'We brought him here, of course. First we learned that he had indeed succeeded in his research project, then that he had managed to conceal an account of his work and a prototype before we got to him, and that he had then sent off a letter to reach you in the States.'

In spite of the stifling warmth of the room, a cold lump — as much rage as fear — began to form in my stomach and the tips of my fingers felt chilled.

'Without delay, we went that same night to collect his papers and the prototype. But either Marshall was lying, which was inconceivable, or we had misunderstood him for we found nothing. When we returned to the House to try to clarify matters we found it was too late. He was dead.'

'How did he die?' I asked in a voice whose calmness astounded me.

Leighton frowned. 'In some way he tricked the man who was

supposed to be keeping an eye on him — he was believed to be unconscious — he made a dash for it, managed to reach the landing at the top of the stairs in the hall before two of the others caught up with him. In the struggle that followed he somehow fell or was pushed over the balustrade and dropped twenty feet to the floor below. Even then he might have escaped with a broken limb. As it was — ' he rubbed his bearded chin in quite obvious exasperation — 'he broke his neck.'

I glanced at Miss Cornelius. She was listening with all the excitement one might have expected if Leighton had been describing how a flying pebble had chipped the paint on his Zephyr.

Leighton shrugged. 'Our only hope, after that, was the letter to you.'

It made sense. 'So you tried to get it back,' I said quietly. For the second time, Leighton frowned.

'Oh dear me no. We intended no such thing. We've been waiting very impatiently for you to receive it and act upon it.'

'But you searched my flat —' I broke off, stopped by the blank look on Leighton's face. For the first time Miss Cornelius looked one hundred per cent alert.

'Searched your flat, Arnott?' He cocked his head to one side as I kept silent. 'Well, well. That's something we'll have to take up later. Yes, indeed.' His eyes met the woman's before returning to study my face. 'No, we wanted you to lead us to the correct spot since according to Marshall, you would understand. You know, we were really worried as the days went on and no letter arrived. And now,' he bit his lip, 'we're still worried for you went straight to the place we searched already, the place where we found nothing.'

He paused. 'I wonder if you've been stringing us along, Arnott, after all. Have you?'

Again I found myself trying to work out too many things at once. Leighton's account had a ring of truth about it, whatever the reality and ramifications of ISGAR. If they really knew what Johnny had been after, then for their own safety as much as for what it could do for them, they had to get it. A sudden nausea hit me and I knew my forehead was damp. I was next on the list. I looked at Leighton.

'Well,' he was saying, 'we'll have to find out, shan't we? In the meantime I want you to listen very carefully to a tape recording. It should interest you. Margaret, would you switch on, please. the last tape.'

I watched Miss Cornelius uncurl and cross to a small table by the wall, carrying a large Grundig tape-recorder. From a drawer in the table she took a spool which she deftly fitted on to the machine. A sharp click heralded the slow revolution of the spools. She returned to her armchair, sat down and looked at me.

A voice I had never expected to hear again spoke, a voice barely recognisable, slurred, crushed but still understandable. In answer to Leighton's sharp, goading question, 'What is your name,?' the weary voice, after a pause that seemed to last for aeons, said, 'John Stanhope Marshall.'

'Good! I see we can continue our conversation. You have told us that you hid the account of your work and the prototype. That is so?'

'That . . . is . . . so.'

'Where did you hide them?' A long pause. 'Answer me. Where did you hide these things?'

'In the ground.'

'The ground? Do you mean you buried them?'

'Yes.'

'Where? Where did you bury them?'

'Under the slaughter stone circle.'

'The slaughter stone circle?' A pause. 'Is the slaughter stone circle one of the group of circles on Machrie Moor?'

'Yes.'

'Which one?'

'The circle with only one slab still standing.'

'And the slaughter stone. What is it?'

'A fragment of sandstone lying on the ground near the circle centre.'

'How does one recognise it?'

'It has six parallel grooves in it.'

'Is your work buried under the slaughter stone?'

'Yes.'

'At what depth?'

'Two feet.'

I sat crouched forward, in a frozen agony of concentration as the magnetic oxide coated ribbon on which a man's last words had found a permanent record slowly unwound. Leighton's probing voice resumed its interrogation.

'Does anyone else know where your work is buried?'

'Not yet.'

'But . . . You mean, you've told someone? Or you've sent word to someone?'

'Yes.'

'How?'

'I wrote a letter to Roger Arnott. . . ' My sense of horror deepened as the questioner with clinical skill extracted from Johnny's mind the way in which he had sent off the airmail letter, the address it had been sent to, various particulars about me and the fact that I could interpret the letter's cryptic directions and recover his work. As the last muttered answer died away, Leighton strode across to the recorder, switched it off and turned back to me, an expectant light in his eyes.

'Now, Arnott.'

A sheet of white-hot rage and hatred exploded within me such as I've experienced only twice before in my life. The sheer outrage, the complete disregard for human suffering or the sanctity of human life, a picture of Laura as I had last seen her, the sound of that limping, hesitant voice on the tape, Leighton's smug, man-of-power face all combined to bring me to my feet, shaking uncontrollably.

'You bastard! You egotistical murdering little bastard!'

His face flushed and I felt a sudden savage glee to see fear in it. But in some way, a bell-push perhaps, a signal must have been given for the door swung back and Cain and Abel were in the room, poised and anticipating whatever move I might make. And behind them a young man with carefully waved fair hair entered. In his hand he held a brown doctor's bag. His interested eyes met mine and he quietly closed the door behind him. Miss Cornelius quite slowly rose, her attention now on Leighton. I found I was breathing through my mouth as if I had been running.

'I was going to give you the opportunity to join us, Arnott,' Leighton said in precise, controlled tones, 'but I see that you wouldn't. You weren't very wise — was he Margaret?' Margaret said nothing. She was a great one for spectating. The others waited. Leighton under-scored his point. 'In fact you've stumbled about in all this in the most fatuous way and shown how essentially stupid you are.' He paused. 'Well, now you'll let us know what exactly Marshall told you in his letter. We'll also find out how much you know about Marshall's work and what you meant by your cryptic accusation that we searched your flat. And also what you've done with the letter. You wouldn't happen to have it on you, would you?'

He read my face and smiled. 'I believe you have. How very accommodating of you. Now! Where did Marshall hide his stuff?'

'I haven't the faintest idea.'

He nodded. 'And what do you know about Marshall's work?'

'Nothing.'

'What made you think we searched your flat?'

My mind assessed and re-assessed the situation in a frantic effort to see a way out. Time was almost up. 'I must have been dreaming.'

Leighton played it out to the end, quite obviously tasting and relishing his mastery of the scene.

'And the letter?'

'Here it is.' I drew it from my inside pocket, held it out to Leighton and as he automatically reached for it I gripped his wrist and jerked. He shot past me into the armchair. With the leverage, I leaped for the door in the wild hope that I could dodge through and reach the corridor. Cain and Abel, if taken just a little by surprise, still had plenty of time to grab me. Like a sack of oats I was dragged round to face Leighton again. He straightened up, drew a deep gasping breath, then smoothed back his dishevelled grey hair before stooping to pick up the letter. He gave me one furious glance before reading it. Finally he looked up, obviously puzzled. To Miss Cornelius, he said: 'It's just what Marshall told us.'

She bit her lower lip but said nothing. Leighton tapped the letter with his forefinger. 'I think explanations are in order, Arnott. Yes, indeed.'

With a quick jerk of his head he signalled to the pair whose fingers were biting into my wrists and biceps. The young man dragged a solid, dark-oak chair out from the wall to the middle of the room and stepped back. The others forced me into it. The young man helped them to manoeuvre my jacket off before cinching straps he took from the bag round my ankles and wrists. All three stepped back. I strained my neck round, every nerve raw with tension, my heart thudding, the tall-ceilinged room, the glowing fire, the handsome furniture and the looming faces of its occupants perceived with an intensity heightened by apprehension. And yet disbelief vied with my terror, disbelief that the civilised world-line of my existence could have sideslipped me into this nightmare situation.

Leighton's voice brought my attention back to him.

'Right. Wait outside.'

Cain and Abel nodded and left the room. My mind said: 'They don't know what Johnny created and he doesn't want them to know. It'll be kept among the top brass.'

'Put a new tape on, Margaret, please.' She crossed behind Leighton. His eyes searched my face.

'In the old days, Arnott, in the days of the Gestapo, even the most determined man could be broken in time. You doubtless know the sort of simple but effective mechanical and electrical gadgets their interrogation teams employed.'

Inside my skin, I cringed as memories crowded in upon me of accounts I had read of the nauseating obscenities practised by Himmler's psychopaths in the rue des Saussaies and scores of other ante-rooms to Hell all over Europe.

'But of course it often took time to loosen a stubborn man's tongue' — no time at all with me, I thought frenziedly, if only I knew something — 'and he very often concocted the most ingenious lies to stop further applications of these gadgets.' As I will, I promised. 'Fortunately, however, science comes to our aid, transforming a messy unreliable time-consuming process to a fast, precise, dependable procedure.' He paused. 'In cases such as yours, we have found it useful to employ a drug rather similar to sodium pentathol in its effects but quicker acting. It is also much more reliable in bypassing the ego and will to reach into the memory.' He smiled briefly. 'So you can relax. It's all quite, quite painless. In fact there won't even be a jag. Monty is using a pressure hypodermic that shoots the drug right through the

92

skin without using a needle. We cannot leave any suspicious punctures on you.'

He turned his head. 'Right, Monty.'

So this is what they did to Johnny, I thought dismally, conscious of a craven sense of relief. The young man lifted the scuffed brown bag on to the occasional table beside the Grundig, opened it and brought out a syringe. Miss Cornelius dragged the left arm of my shirt up to my shoulder, while I hoped to hell that my sub-conscious had not made better sense of Johnny's letter than my conscious mind. Monty pressed the cold nozzle of the syringe into my arm and immediately I felt the dull load of the drug invade my tissues.

Leighton watched keenly.

'Thank you, Monty.' Dismissed, the young man replaced the hypodermic in his bag, snapped it shut, grinned at me, and left the room. Resident doctor? I wondered. As I watched the door close after him, I experienced the first effects of the drug. A warm, comfortable feeling of detachment pervaded my body and mind, wrapping me in a careless, spectator-like state of limbo from which I distantly viewed the action as if watching unfolding hypnagogic hallucinations. I heard someone else answering Leighton's questions, giving my name, my age, various personal details, my views on Johnny's discovery, his letter, an account of how I had been followed and my flat searched, over and over again, back and forth, until the veils lifted gradually and I returned along the widening tunnel and I finally realised the drug had worn off.

The Grundig had been switched off. Cigarette smoke wreathed the room, hanging in a fog that stung my nostrils. Leighton, an expression of frustration tightening his face, was pacing up and down. Miss Cornelius, looking tired and unhappy, sat on the sofa. I suddenly realised my hands and feet were numb and my body felt clammy with cold sweat. All in all I doubted if I could stand if I was released from the chair.

'I can't understand it,' Leighton muttered. 'He doesn't know a thing.'

The hoarseness of my voice surprised me. 'Perhaps you asked the wrong questions.'

They stared at me. Without warning, Leighton strode across to me and backhandedly smashed me across the face. Even as my eyes stung and watered, the room dissolved into a shimmering liquid veil and my right cheek burned, I felt a sudden vicious joy at the defeat his tantrum revealed. He stepped back.

'Let me give you something to think about for the rest of the night, Arnott. First thing in the morning we will take you to the top of the Doon and stage a little accident. In fact, you'll be found at the foot of the cliff, having fallen over the edge. We will leave it to the police to decide whether you fell or committed suicide.'

'Two accidents in the same place? They'll find that difficult to swallow.'

'At first, perhaps, but not for ever. I can see the picture. You came down here again; you went over to the Doon again and then — well, either you fell or jumped. It'll make a nice unsolved mystery for the Sunday newspapers in years to come. The police may wonder, but what can they discover?'

The question was indeed unanswerable. Leighton's eyes held mine. 'In any case I shall prefer doing it this way. Somehow it appeals to the craftsman in me. In point of fact, Arnott, I'd like to take you over there now but we must wait until the marks of the straps have worn off, mustn't we?' He signed to Miss Cornelius. She must have pressed a button, for the door opened and Cain and Abel came into the room.

'Give him his jacket and put him in the basement.'

Once on my feet, I found I was steadier than I had anticipated. My face still throbbed and I felt desperately thirsty. As Cain and Abel propelled me to the door, Leighton hoped I'd sleep soundly. I found I was all out of exit lines so said nothing. They took me along the corridor, down the main staircase, round behind it and down an uncarpeted basement flight, our feet clattering on the stone steps. A stout wooden door was opened and they pushed me into a black, unlit cellar-like compartment. The door slammed behind me, cutting off all light and I heard the metal thud of bolts being thrown over and a key scraping round in the lock.

I stood still in the blackness. As the pupils of my eyes gradually expanded to their fullest extent, I detected a faint patch of starlight high up on the wall facing me. The accommodation of my vision improved to the extent that I could see dimly a long low shape that on tactual investigation turned out to be a camp bed with a foam rubber mattress and one blanket. I also found a zinc bucket by kicking it. The symbolism didn't appeal to me. When I shuffled across the room to the window I saw that there were four vertical iron bars just beyond the dust-surfaced glass. I had no difficulty in reaching up and opening the narrow window which hinged upwards but experiment soon disclosed to me the Victorian solidity with which the rusty bars were anchored into the stonework. And beyond them a wooden hatch had been bolted into place. It was through a thin crack in this that the light came.

I brushed the flakes of rust off my hands and returned to the bed. Lying full length on it, I tried to think but evidently the drug had after-effects for the next thing I knew I was wakened by the muffled chorus of birds triggered off by the increasing light. I leapt off the bed in alarm, crossed to the cellar window and tried to peer out. The bars however prevented me from putting an eye near enough the crack to get any field of vision and I returned to the bed. I lay down again and studied the crack pattern in the ceiling. It was another eighty minutes before I heard the bolts being withdrawn and the door being unlocked. Springing to my feet, I faced the door as it swung back.

Leighton and Monty stood there. The younger man held an automatic pistol pointing straight at my chest.

'All right, Arnott,' said Leighton. 'Time to go.'

7 Victim Running

The Armstrong-Siddeley stood on the gravel path in front of the house. Behind it was the green Zephyr, the early morning sunshine sparkling off its bodywork. Beside it stood Cain and Abel, and Miss Cornelius. Both men wore windcheaters and American baseball-type caps. They also carried bags of golfclubs. Miss Cornelius wore white shorts and a heavy grey pullover over a blue shirt. A red hairband contrasted with her blonde hair. She rested the base of a golfbag on the gravel. When she saw me she smiled nicely.

Leighton's hand gripped me above the elbow as I hesitated. 'You can drive,' he said. 'I'll be beside you. Monty will be behind you. And they'll be in the Zephyr right behind us.' He grinned as he caught me eyeing them. 'Oh yes, they're coming with us to see you off. They might even have a game afterwards.' He jerked my arm forward. 'Get in.'

I got in. He took the front passenger seat. Monty, also in sports attire, was now in the rear passenger seat behind me. In the rear mirror I met his eyes and his mouth acted out a smile. I could see the other three getting into the Zephyr.

'All right. Start moving. Take the coast road. And not too fast.' Leighton pretended to recall our purpose. 'Ah, but then, I'm sure you're in no hurry.'

I made no reply. As I swung the old car down the drive and turned left on to the main road I was too busy thinking. Or trying to think for all I seemed to achieve was a series of fragmentary irrelevant snatches of thought that aroused a feeling of anger within me that I couldn't do better. In the early morning the road was deserted. Heavy banks of clouds covered most of the sky and there was a chill to the air. I shivered.

'Looks like rain,' Leighton said.

Monty agreed. 'We might have to miss that game. You've never been interested, Kenneth?'

'Never found the time.'

'That's a pity. It gets a real grip of you, you know. You lie awake at night wondering why you played a bad game. Wondering if you'll manage to correct that slice. Incidentally, Margaret's game has improved a lot. Of course she gets a lot more practice than us. Have you ever played, Arnott?'

I was glad and a little surprised that my voice was steady.

'I used to. But not for a number of years.' And never again, I told myself.

The Zephyr sauntered along, a hundred yards to the rear. Leighton remarked conversationally: 'I wonder would you be inclined to take the car over the cliff and kill all three of us if we'd been on the coast road between Blackwaterfoot and Corriecravie?'

He smiled as I kept silent. 'Somehow I don't think so. For one thing you don't really believe yet it's going to happen and for another, we might not all have been killed — such accidents have such uncertain consequences, don't you think. In any case, if you'll pardon the cliché, while there's life there's hope. That is the carrot that will take the donkey right up to the edge of Drumadoon.'

I wished to heaven he'd shut up and let me think. But even if he did, I had no real expectation of using my brain profitably. The scenery, the fields, the farm-houses, the rolling brown and green slopes of the Moss away to the left, the grey waters of the Sound with the lowering moisture-laden cloudbanks dragged at my body's attention as if it had a sensibility far greater than that of the ego and, in anticipation of its destruction in the near future, was solacing itself by storing sense data from its peaceful surroundings.

We began to turn downhill towards the coast. The whine of the engine as I changed it into third gear increased my tension. Time was running out and I hadn't a coherent thought in my head.

'Turn right at the foot of the hill, Arnott,' said Leighton. I did so and began the last part of the journey along the short, narrow road between the rocky shore and the row of trim houses that leads to the Blackwaterfoot and Shiskine Golf Club House. The gravel parking lot was empty.

'Don't park here,' Leighton ordered. 'Go on.'

At about ten miles an hour, the Armstrong-Siddeley jolted along the track, the sand hissing beneath its wheels, the occasional pebble striking the car's underside with a clatter. I glanced once at Leighton and found him gazing fixedly at me, openly watchful now. His left hand now rested in his lap and held a small automatic pistol.

'Just before we turn inland, take the car off the track. There's a parking place there.'

I did so. The small sandy clearing was hidden from view by large grass-topped dunes. I switched off the ignition. After some ten seconds or so, the Zephyr pulled in beside us. Some spots of rain appeared on the windscreen and I noted how dark and choppy the sea had become.

The other car's doors slammed and Cain and Abel and Miss Cornelius retrieved their golfbags from its capacious boot. They waited.

'Get out,' said Leighton. Before I could shut the door he added: 'Take the ignition key. And lock the doors after us.' Monty took his clubs from Cain. He looked at the sky.

'Going to be a heavy shower,' he remarked. Leighton inspected the cloud-banks to the north-west. 'It'll hold for fifteen minutes.' He turned to the other trio. 'You three cross the links to the Doon and get to the top. We'll follow you in three minutes.' They left, Cain first and then Abel and Miss Cornelius together. Leighton turned back to me. I noticed he had his gun in his pocket. More spots of rain hit my face.

'Sorry the weather's deteriorating, Arnott,' he apologised, as if he was in charge of it. 'If you like, you can look upon it as a personal example of the pathetic fallacy. Now let me put you in the picture. The others, who in effect are behaving like Chesterton's postman — you remember the story? — will park their clubs at the foot of the Doon once they're across the links. Then they'll climb it and spread out along the two ends of the path on the sea-face and the entrance on the land-slope. We will go on to the top and go to the edge. When they confirm that there are no onlookers — at this time of the morning I'd be most surprised if there were — Monty and I will help you to have your little accident.'

His face hardened. 'Be very careful, Arnott. Any nonsense on your part on the way up and we'll put a bullet through you. It'll make things rather more awkward for us and I'd certainly be disappointed for I'm looking forward to seeing you go off the edge.' His mouth twisted. 'It should take you three seconds to fall, I imagine. Not a long time, but what you might call a lifetime. Now get going.'

When we came out between the dunes, the rising wind whipped at us. Leighton and Monty followed me. We crossed the stile and began the climb. The rain was slightly heavier now and I felt numb mentally and physically, apart from a core of fear and resentment that I was being forced to climb up this hill to my death without being able to do anything about it. A certain insidious aura of unreality began to invest my mind and I fought against it. I glanced back and down. They were being careful, remaining close but not close enough for any move of desperation on my part to succeed. I felt my heart thudding and I paused. The other two seemed glad enough of a rest. Away over to the right the storm-clouds were so low now that the hills were completely misted. It was getting so dark that lights appeared in some of the distant Blackwaterfoot houses. The bulk of the Doon hid everything to the north-west where the weather was coming from so that at the moment we were comparatively sheltered.

Leighton evidently thought I was putting it off — as indeed I was — for he shouted at me to go on. I climbed upwards along the path and the last moments passed and we were coming up over the rough shoulder on to the top about two hundred and fifty feet from the sheer drop that was our goal. Ahead, the rock outcrops thrust themselves in tumbled and weathered confusion above the lumpy tufts of heather and grass to heights of five or more feet. And some three or four seconds before Leighton and Monty saw it, still behind and below me, I saw and appreciated the weather front sweeping towards us across the water. Before ten seconds had passed it was upon us.

The clouds now sped by only feet above our heads, black, twisting, rolling masses that discharged a sheet of water as if they had been suspended polythene reservoirs ripped to shreds. The sea itself, before the black wall of rainwater engulfed us and destroyed visibility, foamed and surged as the wind gusts whipped it to fury.

Now, I told myself. I plunged forward into the storm, leaping and twisting among the rock-masses, slipping on the soaking vegetation, my back shrinking in anticipation of the bullet that would bite into it. Even with the wind's roar I heard Leighton shout something and twice I heard rather than saw a bullet star rock fragments from beside me. I sprinted blindly onwards, dodging and gasping, in the direction I had last seen the edge. Once I crashed face on into a block that I didn't see until it was too late. Almost before I knew it I was on the brink of the huge step I had aimed for, an uneven, heather and grass-covered rock ledge some ten to twenty feet wide and some five to thirty feet below the general level of the Doon top. Beyond it lay the total blackness of the abyss in front of the great columns of porphyritic structure that formed the cliff-face. At the point I reached, the drop was about seven feet. I leaped down on to the edge and sprawled there for a moment's respite. I found I was panting like a dog and my mouth burned with a metallic taste.

I scraped rain-water from my streaming face and licked my hand while I found myself thinking idiotically in the mock-enthusiastic tones of a quizmaster: you've won half a minute; *now* will you try for *life*? I began to scramble through the downpour along the ledge between the streaming rocks and tossing, clammy wet ferns with smoky wisps of cloud writhing past me. From experience I knew these storms couldn't sustain their fury for more than a few minutes — Cain and Abel would keep their places at the ends of the cliff path; Miss Cornelius, Leighton and Monty had me between them and the drop and they'd be closing in as fast as they could.

I scuttled on, bent almost double, in the direction of the Sentinel, the isolated, nearly entire pillar of rock at the south-west corner of the Doon overlooking the golf-links far beneath. Jumping over small ledges and dodging single blocks, I reached my objective in total amazement at having escaped a broken leg so far. My memory hadn't failed me. A cleft split the cliff-face driving in a wedge of space that, fifteen or so feet wide at the top, shrank to vanishing point a hundred feet down where the vertical columns of the precipice met the great talus-slope of fallen and shattered blocks that descended steeply another hundred feet to the rocky shore.

In my right and cautious mind I couldn't have done it. Now I clambered down the almost vertical cleft-side, clinging to tufts of soaking grass, gripping rocks fiercely, my feet slipping and slithering more often than not, spurts of water from the Doon jetting over my shoulders and running up my sodden sleeves. A spool of snapshot memories was taken: the crack pattern in a slab with two heather sprigs coming from it, the splash of a quicksilver runnel of water on a rock by my head, the soft, cold, plastic feel of mud, the warm, salt taste of my sweat and the slick, soapy feel of blood on my cut face. I hit the top of the talus-slope and scrambled down the multi-shaped slabs and rubble to the beach. The mist was lifting and the force of wind and rain was markedly less. I glanced up at the looming mass of the Doon and was horrified to be able to see the cliff top. With a long sobbing breath that hurt my chest, I sprinted over the pebble banks towards the ragged, wave-worked basaltic dikes that would give me cover.

Once over the fence between shore and golf-links, I dropped behind a dike and lay flat, gasping, the pungent smells of rotting seaweed and the wet tweed of my jacket mingled in my nostrils. I had no time to spare, however. Slowly I raised my head above the top of the dike and scanned the summit of the Doon. I froze. One of the men — I couldn't tell which — was beating his way along the edge. The others would be somewhere on the plateau, searching every crevice and fern patch able to hide me. A last flurry of wind and rain spurred me into action. I began running along the rocky shore, keeping well under the dike and dune edge of the golf course on the side away from the Doon, trying to cut round the links to the small parking place where the cars had been left. The third of a mile over rough ground in soaking wet clothes left me winded. Just before I turned the last corner I burrowed into the sandy side of a grass-topped dune. If Leighton had suspected I had slipped through he would have sent someone straight back across the links to guard the cars. Where would he stand, knowing I was unarmed? The cars were in the hollow with dunes all about except on the shore side and the opposite side leading to the track.

I deliberately took some deep breaths and used my dishcloth of a handkerchief to wipe my face. With the handkerchief still in my hand, I noticed a small bank of pebbles. Quickly I selected an apple-sized stone of grey granite, rough, but rounded by the sea. Back to the stone age. I scrambled up the dune, my hands and feet scoring deep cavities in its dark-brown sandy sides and looked gingerly over the grassy edge. There he was, either Cain or Abel, standing on top of the Zephyr, arms akimbo, legs apart, gazing up at the Doon. His shoes were on a level with my head, a gap of six feet separating the grassy top from the car. I ducked lower and spent half a minute of the little time I had left watching him. He was consistent. He rotated slowly like a lighthouse beam every twelve seconds or so and I knew this was the only chance I had. I dug in my toe-holds in the sand to firm them up and gripped the grass with my left hand and the rock with my right.

When his back was to me, I swung myself up over the edge, sprang to my feet, darted forward and leaped the gap. He was swinging round in alarm, his lips parted, right hand diving for his pocket when I collided with him. At one and the same moment I felt my feet slip on the wet roof, heard him gasp, held his gun-arm trapped against his body with my left arm and felt us hurtle back to half-fall off the Zephyr roof over the three foot gap between the two cars and land against the Siddeley's roof edge with a sound between a thud and a crack. He gave a queer half-yell, half-gasp and then we dropped down between the cars to the puddled ground. I remembered the stone still gripped in my right hand and raised it. His body crushed my arm which still imprisoned the gun in his pocket, his brown, staring eyes glared up at me while his mouth lay wide open. The ever-ready camera of my mind registered his well-filled teeth. Quite suddenly, just as I began to strike downwards, I realised he wasn't struggling. I hesitated. He seemed paralysed and I pulled my arm free. He made no resistance when I dragged his hand from his pocket, prised the blue steel automatic from it and threw it away under the car. He still made no move and an appalling thought occurred to me. Dropping the rock, I unzipped his sodden windcheater and felt for his heartbeat through his wet shirt. There was none. He was dead.

I remember my next thoughts were: Good God, his back. It broke when we hit the edge of the Siddeley's roof. Is there a doctor in Blackwaterfoot? You incredible idiot, he tried to kill you. The others will be back at any moment.

I rose and stumbled up the slope nearest the Doon. I saw one figure on the lower slopes at the old entrance between the ruined stone age battlements and another coming over the links. The nearer figure — I thought it was Monty — began to run. I slid back down, unlocked the Siddeley's door and inserted the ignition key. Then I sprinted round the bonnet of the car to the driver's door of the Zephyr. It was locked. They all were. I didn't waste time searching the body sprawled between the cars. Picking up the rock I'd discarded, I smashed the quarter-light window on the near side, inserted my hand and pulled up the black locking knob. I opened the door, leant in and gasped with relief when I found the bonnet release knob under the dash. I raised the bonnet and within seven seconds had torn away as many leads. Before making for the driver's seat of the Siddeley, I closed the Zephyr bonnet. Even that might win me a few seconds.

Just before I pressed the starter the shattering thought hit me — supposing I *now* find the rain-storm has wet the plugs. It hadn't. The engine fired immediately and I reversed back on to the track, skidded to a halt in a change to forward gear before roaring away. In the rear mirror Monty appeared over the dune, hesitated and then was too far behind to do any damage.

I now had to get off the island. What I didn't know was how many people they had available to them but I did know that they would expend any effort to kill me. But certainly not in public unless it could be made to appear a natural or accidental death. Unpleasantly plausible pictures rose before me: a jostle in a crowd and — 'my friend seems to have fainted. Could you help me carry him to my car.' Or — 'I just couldn't avoid him: he fell right in front of the car.'

I had at most five minutes before Leighton got to a phone. But unless he had anyone over on the other side of the island, I stood a good chance of getting there before them. I might indeed just make the next boat. And there was a possibility that I had immobilised his total force behind me. I passed the junction that led to Machrie and soon after crossed the Blackwaterfoot Bridge before turning sharp left at the Kinloch Hotel away from the shore. Half a minute later I had taken the left hand fork leading to Shiskine and was driving as fast as I dared towards the String Road. The weather had continued to improve and the air was now clean with that super-transparent quality it often gets after such a storm. Kintyre was clear and I supposed the storm by now would be battering the south-east part of the island. My clothes felt clammy and stuck both to me and the leather seat. My trousers were torn at both knees and were stained with mud and vegetation. I had a sore cheekbone and my left shin burned and throbbed where I had scraped it in the fall between the cars. But my pulse was steadier and I had lost the sheer outraged near-panic that had possessed me from the moment I darted forward at the top of the Doon. Close down adrenalin production, open up cortex, I thought. But the respite in the eye of the storm was short-lived.

As I neared the pillar post-box at the junction of the Shiskine and Machrie Roads, a grey Minivan catapulted up the Machrie Road from the Glaistir Bridge. Even as I rammed down the accelerator I remembered a similar van in the yard at Carradale House and the computer in my mind gave its comments: distance from Carradale House along the Machrie Road to postbox is three miles — distance from the Doon along the Shiskine Road is six miles — they must have belted along — Leighton must have phoned within three minutes.

The needle climbed to sixty-five as I dived down the last slope and ripped past the stone pillar box on to the String. My lead increased as the Mini slowed to make the left hand turn. But I couldn't hold it on the twisting narrow road for the Mini was not only more manoeuvrable than the ton and a half of Armstrong-Siddeley but also had a better driver. In the next thirty seconds the lead dwindled noticeably even before we began the climb up the String with its sharp corners that would certainly let them get right behind me. They couldn't pass if I kept to the road centre and they couldn't tumble the heavy Siddeley off the road to go crashing down the sloping sides of the Glen into the river but I'd no doubt they could put a bullet in me or a tyre before we reached the top.

My logic overcame the seductive illusion of security the car interior gave me and at the last possible moment I jammed both feet on clutch and brake. The speed fell from seventy to well under thirty in a scream of fusing rubber and in the rear mirror I saw the Mini shorten the gap by eighty feet. I raised my feet, stopped fighting the wheel, swung it hard left to the full extent of its lock and felt the big car swing off the road on two wheels and dive down the steep, almost hidden farm road leading to Monyquil. In the mirror I saw the Mini shoot past, its driver obviously braking. Feeling sweat bands trickle down my forehead, I drove along the stony track, crossed the narrow wooden bridge over the Machrie water with a rattling of planks then followed the track between the fields up to the farm house. The Mini appeared two hundred yards behind me. I put the Siddeley on to the second bridge over the Garbh Allt stream, ran it along to a farm gate and stopped. If they had a rifle I was done for. I jumped out, climbed the gate and sprinted for the rising grassy slopes that bordered the stream. Breasting the first rise I turned and looked backwards and downwards.

The grey Mini had stopped behind the Siddeley. Two men had got out. A third stayed in the driver's seat. After a short discussion the two started off after me. Neither had rifles.

I began to move upwards again over the uneven tufted grass slope. The going was comparatively easy, the springy vegetation letting one's feet sink in until the tufts came to mid-shin. There were bog-wet patches and quite soon my shoes, socks and the legs of my trousers were as sodden as before. I found myself settling down to a fast, bouncing pace determined by the nature of the terrain and my need to keep at least three hundred yards ahead of my pursuers. They tried to run several times and I had to do likewise but the ground soon discouraged such attempts. They were now committed, as I had intended, to tiring me or sneaking up when the surface permitted.

By the time we had gone a mile towards the north, I could tell which of the two was the greater danger. The smaller and stockier man wore a neat dark blue lounge suit; he tended to lag behind and once I saw him sit on a rock outcrop, shoulders hunched, his hands on his knees, for the best part of a minute while he got his breath back. The other in striped tee-shirt and faded blue jeans, was in better condition. I continued to climb, still following the burn, moving almost due north towards the lower, rock-bestrewn slopes of Ben Nuis.

By now I felt hot and semi-exhausted, my shirt and singlet sticking to the small of my back while streams of sweat coursed down my burning face. The only sound I heard was the regular heavy in-and-out breath in my open mouth, as if some phantom doctor accompanying me kept ordering me to take deep breaths. I wondered what the third man in the Mini was doing. Probably reporting back to Leighton. With that thought I changed direction slightly, now aiming for the western shoulder of Ben Nuis. The ground began to steepen and more and more of it became composed of outcrop and broken rock with bell heather, blaeberry plants and tough knotted grass between. I had now come two and a half miles and climbed a thousand feet from the place where I'd abandoned the Armstrong-Siddeley.

Glancing back, I saw that Tee-shirt was attempting a spurt. He managed to close the gap to one hundred and fifty yards before a faint shout from Lounge Suit, now three hundred yards behind, made him slow up and sink on to a rock. I kept on, now scrambling over the lower part of the shoulder of the Ben, its huge granite bulk heaping up to my right. To the left the ground fell away sharply down to the distant Iorsa Water in its meanders over the sea-green bottom of Glen Iorsa. Beyond the Glen, Chalmadale and Ben Bharrain soared up, blotting out the far distant Mull of Kintyre. To the south-west, the Mull was visible, down past Davaar Island to where Sanda Isle lay darkly on the grey-blue horizon.

Tee-shirt was waiting until Lounge Suit caught up. Very gratefully, I slowed up, just moving forward, for my heart was pounding and I would have given anything to lie prone for five minutes. I transferred my wallet, pen, diary and keys to my trousers pockets and threw away my tweed jacket. My tie went into my pocket. I should have done it when I left the car.

I was now climbing up into the bleak, granite heart of the island where the great ridges and peaks rise in their most impressive aspects, desolate, tumbled, old. The silence was broken only by my harried breathing or the sudden startled whirring flutter of the occasional grouse's wings or the cold splash of a spring tumbling down over wet lichened rocks on the side of Ben Nuis. For mile upon mile on all sides there was not a single human habitation. Twice I spotted herds of red-coated deer. In one case, a solitary stag, his antlers held high, lorded it amid a dozen hinds. The second group consisted of thirty or more stags.

I glanced back. Leighton's men were on the move again. I began to work my way northwards along the difficult forty-five degree slope of Ben Nuis. The whole slope consisted of a semi-scree of irregular, granite blocks from loaf-sized cubic boulders to megalithic slabs, all jumbled together as they had broken and avalanched down the slope. There were patches a few yards across where decomposed granite rubble and rotting vegetation had enabled a tough matting of thickly-woven heather and grass to grow over the naked rock.

It took an hour to cover just over a mile of this treacherous ground in my exhausted state. My pursuers, I was satisfied to see, were now at least three hundred yards back and still keeping to my path. This they had to do since they had no idea whether I meant to strike up the slope of Ben Nuis or veer north-west downwards to the floor of Glen Iorsa in a desperate effort to break out to Loch Ranza. I felt grateful that I had explored these moors and mountains as a boy and was still fond of walking.

I now dropped a couple of hundred feet in the next half mile where the western slope of Ben Nuis becomes the western slope of Ben Tarsuinn. The ground was flatter in front of me but shot up more steeply to the right in great granite sheets, eroded and split by millenia of weathering, to the saddle between the Bens. I braced myself for I was nearing the point where I hoped to get rid of Tee-shirt and Lounge Suit. Roger the Dodger, I thought. I cheered myself a little by considering their quandary. If Leighton and Co. hadn't found the gun I had thrown away, they had to assume I was armed. Tee-shirt and Lounge Suit had probably been warned about this and it could be the reason they hadn't closed in yet, though I suspected and hoped it simply meant that they were even more exhausted than I was. They also faced the fact that although their Mini driver knew I had lit out for the hills, he had no idea what area I was in now. I stumbled, almost fell and recovered myself. Again I had a sudden terrifying vision of breaking a leg and lying there while they closed in to finish me off. I felt sickness well up within me and a metallic taste contaminated my mouth when I recalled coming across a dead sheep on these very same hills years ago after the carrion crows had been at it for a week. I steadied myself and looked round.

Ahead of me the giant shoulder of Ben Tarsuinn rose, encumbered with thousands of granite blocks. To the left it swept downwards more and more steeply to the Iorsa Valley. To the right it rose five hundred feet to the summit, 2,700 feet high. Beyond it I knew the ground fell sharply into a hollow at the base of A'Chir Ridge with a visible path running up the side to the top of the jagged, deeply-notched ridge.

I stepped across a tiny burn, knelt down and cupped my hands in the freezing water. As I drank, the cold liquid chilling my gullet, the wet from the heather and moss soaked my knees. I glanced back over the dripping bowl of my fingers and saw that they were having another conference. Lounge Suit pointed backwards, Tee-shirt shook his head angrily. By no means an academic discussion. I sat down on a boulder and rested my back against a convenient block behind it. For a few seconds I felt much worse, my legs quivery, my lungs raw, my mouth now an inner core of melting ice in the furnace of my face. I splashed my face with water and wiped it. Sweat started out immediately after. My feet were beginning to hurt and in two places at least developing blisters were heralding their painful advent. I thought I knew the terms of the discussion. If Lounge Suit went back down to Monyquil he could tell the others where we were but (a) it would take *him* — I glanced at my watch — good heavens, at least three hours to deliver the message to Garcia unless they were on their way up and (b) it would diminish their ability to stop me breaking back if I intended to repeat my tactics at the Doon.

My breathing was back to normal. I rose and started off towards the shoulder ahead that ran across my route. I moved steadily until I was on top with the broad ridge surging away up to the peak on my right and could now see down into the gully between Tarsuinn and A'Chir Ridge. I went on, descending fifty feet or so until the shoulder hid me from sight. Immediately it did so I turned right and began to scramble as fast as I could over the green-brown tufts and white-wash hued blocks. I climbed on, rapidly getting more and more exhausted in a supreme effort to reach the top of Ben Tarsuinn before the others came over the ridge. The last two hundred feet almost beat me. I dropped every fifty feet or so on to the nearest granite block to drag oxygen into my tormented lungs before clawing my way upwards again. Still there was no sign of the others. I made a final endeavour and collapsed in the shelter of the gigantic tabular masses of granite that lie sheet upon weathered sheet in great prismatic forms on the edge of the vertical eastern face of Ben Tarsuinn.

By now, I thought, they would be arriving on top of the ridge and would really be in trouble. Apart from the hundreds of blocks I could be hiding behind, they would discover there were three or four widely different routes I could have taken, all of them possessing plenty of cover. If they were townbred, too, as I suspected, the scene before them could only engender confusion and dismay. Beyond A'Chir Ridge a maze of great precipices fell away to the depths from blue-grey towering crests of naked rock crowned with massive blocks, up to ten feet thick, forming tumbled and ruined stone walls. Their confusion would be increased by the way the jagged ridges separated valleys, any one of which could have been my goal, if they could only distinguish the routes over and through the majestic disorder before them.

I guessed they would cast about for a time, very cagily, in case I had any idea of ambushing them. This procedure being fruitless, they might finally agree to split up, one continuing the search (almost certainly Tee-shirt), the other making the irritating and exhausting trek back along the western slopes of Ben Tarsuinn and Ben Nuis before descending across the moor to meet the others coming up from Monyquil. The only possibility that disturbed me was that they might immediately climb after me to the crest of Ben Tarsuinn in an effort to spot me below. I decided it was time to withdraw. Run, do not walk, to the nearest exit.

To anyone reaching the summit of either Ben Tarsuinn or Ben Nuis for the first time, it comes as a surprise to discover that the crest is broad and grassy for most of the way with the living rock bursting through here and there in great heaped up walls and that there is a well-defined though uneven and winding path among these walls and steps. The left hand edge is precipitous, requiring real mountaineering skill; on the right the shoulder dives smoothly over in scree slopes down past the level we had so laboriously worked our way along. I had in fact conned Tee-shirt and Lounge Suit for it is possible to *run* most of the way along the path at the eastern edge of the broad top. If I had been fresh I could by this route have reached the southern end of Ben Nuis ridge in a quarter of an hour or less. In the condition I was in it took longer. I also made full use of the available cover and although I kept looking backwards I saw no sign of pursuit. When I stopped to rest on the steep slope looking north-east over the wide hollow between Ben Nuis and Ben a'Chliabhain I felt certain that I'd left them behind, cloaked with cursing as with a garment.

For two or three minutes I sat there, taking in the spectacular view while I regained composure and tried to programme my next moves in detail. Looking over the green depths of Glen Rosa I could see the whole Brodick plain in miniature, the ochre-yellow strip of beach marking the border between topaz-blue sea and green fields, at right angles to it the minute forms of houses and hotels strung along the road to the pier. Beyond the Clauchland Hills further south, Holy Isle sheltered Lamlash Bay.

A faint whirring noise like a distant egg-beater in action nudged at my attention. It grew louder and I recognised the sound of a helicopter. Suddenly I heard Leighton's voice rerun in my mind: '. . . we . . . can land a helicopter from Abbotsinch if necessary in the grounds.' It could be, I thought, my tension rising again, it could be. I burrowed under the undercut bank of a gully while the noise level rose a few decibels. Finally I spotted the craft chattering across the Moor to the south somewhere above tiny Loch nam Faoileag. It dipped below the horizon as if descending. I began to scramble down the slope keeping near cover as far as possible, following the tiny tributary that enters the other Garbh Allt that is itself a tributary of the Glenrosa Water.

During the next hour before I reached the Rosa Water I had to hide myself three times under the pungent-scented prickly heather or behind rocks when the 'copter chattered into sight across the Ben Nuis-Ben Tarsuinn ridge before swinging back round the range into silence. Its main area of search, however, was obviously the other side of the bens where it had doubtless spotted Tee-shirt and Lounge Suit and presumably the others. By now I had dismissed the possibility of it belonging to either Forestry or Mountain Rescue. I saw it make one final sweep about three forty-five before it flew away across the Firth towards the Ayrshire coast. I gave Leighton an alpha again for his resourcefulness, unprofitable though it had been, and limped on, worried rather than relieved by the helicopter's departure. I thought the situation over once more. Unless Leighton was using all his men on the moor he would have taken the obvious precaution of covering the pier at Brodick and the police station.

I arrived at the first cottages in Glenshurig. Two blisters at least had burst and were pulsing rawly at every step. I had now walked eleven miles and had had nothing to eat for twenty-four hours. Putting on my tie and running a hand through my sweat-sticky hair, I walked on down the hill, crossed the Glenshurig burn and finally reached the junction where the coast road to Corrie breaks away from the String. I found my gaze flicking nervously about me, my nervous tension tautening the nearer I got to the outskirts of Brodick. As I approached the public phone box at Lower Glencloy, I slowed down, trying to discover if it was watched, my mind jittering in indecision. Hell, I told myself, he can't have a regiment at his disposal. A few moments more nerving myself and I entered the box. In the red-painted, musty-smelling glass enclosure I put a three-penny piece in the slot, lifted the phone from its cradle and turned my back to the black mechanism box, the better to see the outside world. I smeared a fresh trickle of sweat from my brow and knew that the inside of the mouth-piece was rapidly becoming beaded with condensed moisture. There was no request from the operator for my number. I waited, jiggled the cradle bar up and down then my ear caught the absence of any 'alive' noise. It was out of order.

I next tried a private house, telling the woman the public phone box was out of order and that my car had gone off the String Road and was in the ditch.

'Come in.' She led me into a brightly-furnished lounge. I lifted the phone and found myself looking at her in enquiry for the same dead feeling met me. I jiggled the pins with no expectation of success.

'I'm afraid your phone is out of order too,' I said and replaced it.

'How strange. I used it only this morning.'

I tried one more house four doors along. Their phone didn't work either and I knew that somehow, with ruthless economy of action, Leighton had arranged that the exchange had had a little accident. A crushing, almost claustrophobic feeling of defeat impinged upon me then I decided to get to the pier and assess the situation there though my hopes in that direction, if nebulous before I tried to phone, were now at vanishing point.

I reached the electric power house on the shore at the side of the pier by making a detour above the village across the Mayish farm lands. Once there I stayed behind the seaweed-covered rocks at the base of the concrete wall bordering the parking lot while I scanned the area. Being off-season now, there were few people present but as the minutes passed, the conclusion was inescapably forced upon me that in my complete inability to recognise Leighton's people — the two men smoking and chatting over by the information booth? — the

111

sandy-haired man reading at the wheel of a parked Anglia? — the three young women who looked as if they were waiting to meet someone off the boat? — I could only become a naked target whenever I tried to cross the pier area and go out on to the pier itself. The utter inability to appeal to anyone there for help bewildered and disheartened me. Could they help me? Would they believe me? And how could I be sure I wasn't approaching Leighton's men? And yet, a small but finite possibility — oh, how small! — remained that Leighton still believed me trapped on the north-east side of Ben Nuis and was deploying every available man in the search. I didn't believe it.

The *Glen Sannox* made the pier. A few cars came off accompanied by a desultory trickle of passengers. Some of the scattered pierhead population greeted them and left with them on foot or by car and bus — only four cars were left in the parking lot, a pale blue Consul, two green Minivans and the Anglia. I found my chest tight and the familiar dull sick feeling loaded my stomach as I debated with myself in another futile attempt to weigh up the probabilities.

Then the door of one of the two Minivans opened and a young woman in a blue windcheater and dark-blue ski-pants got out. She walked over to the pier garage office and turned there. A shock hit me as if a pail of seawater had been thrown over me. It was Claire. When her head turned in my direction, I stood up fully so that my head and shoulders came above the concrete wall. She returned to the van, passed along the side, turned and leaned against the wall, her back to it. She made a business of lighting a cigarette. By the time her lighter was back in her pocket I was behind the section of the wall she leant against. She swung round and looked over without looking down. Her voice came softly to me.

'The back door of the van isn't locked, Roger.'

She moved away. My arms and legs burned with strain and tiredness when I came over the rough concrete wall, my efforts hidden by the Minivan. I opened the door and slipped inside on to the metal floor, a mingled scent of petrol and sacking coming to my nostrils. Behind the seat-backs, tripods, cameras, a case or two and other objects lay. I crouched down as Claire started the engine.

'Get under the sacking, Roger.'

I pulled it over me. The van moved forward. I lay there in foetal position, the rough texture of the canvas scraping my face, and interpreted the sounds that came to me, the pause for the pier-dues transaction, the rumble of the wheels over the pier planking, the bump and clang as the car mounted the ferry ramp, the descent into the hold and the final slow run round the car deck to stop at the rear of the previous vehicle on. Claire switched off the engine, turned her head and said quietly:

'You're late. What kept you?'

8   Gone to Earth

I drew the musty sacking aside and sat up, my back to the side-wall of the van. It felt cold through my shirt.

'I was unavoidably detained.'

'Are you all right?' Her voice was almost a whisper.

'In mint condition.' As I spoke, the computer in my mind, coming unstuck again with the perceptible easing of my tension, was busily tabulating and weighing new hypotheses to account for Claire's presence. The engine-room telegraph gave its ratchety chime and a few moments later the deck began to vibrate. Any reasonable hypothesis had to assume that she was in some way mixed up in it and was certainly not an innocent bystander — the neat business with the Minivan proved that.

'You don't look it,' she said.

'Well, I have been drugged and shot at; I've climbed down a cliff in a thunderstorm and been hunted across the island and have had nothing to eat for twenty-four hours. Oh,' I added as the throbbing in my feet reminded me, 'and my feet are blistered.' And I've killed a man, I thought bleakly.

'There's a small basket beside you. It contains food and a flask of tea.

113

There's also some brandy.' I spotted it and felt myself salivating like one of Pavlov's dogs when the lunchbell sounded. She went on: 'I'm going up to the lounge now. It'll look more natural. Keep down, Roger, in case they've put someone on board. See you at Fairlie.'

She fussed for a moment, collected a purse, then got out and slammed the door behind her. I listened to the sound of her heels against the metal deck until she entered the alley-way leading upstairs, the sounds punctuated by the noise of other car doors closing as their occupants also prepared to go up. Then all I heard was the muted roar of the ventilating fan and the throb of the ship's engines.

I restrained myself from ransacking the basket for thirty minutes, remaining crouched under the sacking for that period, my opinion oscillating between a conviction that my behaviour was a necessary precaution in case Leighton did have someone on board and a self-conscious feeling that I was being unnecessarily windy. In spite of Leighton's own words and the events of the past twenty-four hours, I still found it difficult to believe wholeheartedly that this was no normal academic problem I was assessing but that my life would be chopped short if I reasoned wrongly. And I'm too young to die, the idiot part of my mind added, shocking me with its facile flippancy. For God's sake, I thought, this isn't a game or a film. And interwoven with these iterative thoughts another nasty one kept nudging at me, the possibility that Claire was in with them, that at this very moment she was sitting upstairs with one or more of Leighton's men, laughing at the picture of me crouched in the back of the Minivan, like a fox gone to earth (a fox? — a sheep!), of how she had only to appear at Brodick Pier and I immediately stumbled from cover and docilely clambered into the cage.

I tried to tell myself that they would have grabbed me there and then but inexorably I had to realise that they might feel it would be more convenient if Claire took me back to the mainland to some quiet spot where there would be no witnesses to see my unfortunate demise, as Leighton would undoubtedly phrase it, some quiet spot where my body might never be found. I also tried desperately to convince myself that the personality and character Claire had revealed when we had met before were just not consistent with those displayed by Leighton

114

and his group. And yet I knew with a sinking feeling that although she attracted me so strongly, evoking emotions I believed I had done with and buried in the past, I was still uncertain.

After half an hour on this mental treadmill, I sat up again. I reached across, drew the basket to me and opened it. There were sandwiches, ham, egg and tomato, wrapped neatly in polythene, two oranges and two bananas, a blue-and-white Thermos, a small bottle of Martell Three-Star brandy, plastic containers holding milk and sugar. I had the soapy-smooth glistening polythene off and a ham sandwich between my teeth when the thought that if Claire was with Leighton the food might be drugged locked my jaws. I lowered my hand, separated the top bread slice from the meat and inspected the ham. Nothing to see. I thought: it could be, perhaps I'd better stick to the oranges and bananas: they couldn't be drugged. . . Oh yes, they could be, my clever self said: a hypodermic through the peel or skin. Oh for heaven's sake, I yelled silently. You trust Claire, she wouldn't. . .

I bit into the sandwich and chewed. I unscrewed the thermos top and used it as a cup. I laced the heavily-sweetened tea with brandy. Within ten minutes I had made deep inroads into the provisions and felt much better. Soon I heard Claire's approaching footsteps. The car door was opened, she slipped behind the wheel so that the seat creaked. The door closed.

'All right, Roger?' Her voice was the merest whisper.

'Yes. You pack a nice picnic hamper?'

'Good. Now keep your head down.'

I felt my tension build up again as other car doors slammed and the engine rhythm altered. The Minivan moved forward after a few thousand years (or so it seemed) and without incident went up in the lift, left the *Glen Sannox* and rattled along the pier planks. Once clear of Fairlie, Claire increased speed. I had long since come out of my cocoon of sacking and was sitting up but had no clear view of the route she was taking. About twenty minutes after we left the ship I felt a sudden surge of alarm when she stopped the car. She leaned back.

'No one is following, Roger. You can come into the front seat now. You'll be more comfortable there.' I released my breath.

We started off again. I looked at Claire's profile, at her hands gripping the wheel and I felt my heart leap. She turned her head and grinned at me before concentrating on the road ahead.

'Well, we made it,' she said. She took her left hand off the wheel and briefly gripped my hand before saying, more soberly, 'I didn't really think we would.'

'You know, strangely enough, I had my doubts, too.' I hesitated. 'I take it you didn't just happen to be passing by?'

She flashed me a sympathetic smile. 'Poor Roger. You must be getting thoroughly mixed up with all this cloak and dagger stuff.'

'Yes, that's me,' I replied grimly, 'a thoroughly mixed-up kid. Every time I think I've learned the plot and the rules, they change.' Again I hesitated. 'You haven't answered my question, Claire.'

'No, I didn't just happen to be passing by. I was hoping to get you out.'

I shifted my feet to ease the flesh-raw pain from my blisters. So she wasn't an innocent bystander. Then whose side was she on and how much did she know? And — a mental analogy to the physical pain I was feeling — did she meet me deliberately that day on the Moor and from then on simply play me like a fish on a line? And how did she learn I needed help, if she wasn't in with Leighton?

'All right,' I said evenly, 'how did you know I was in trouble?'

She was silent while the Mini ripped along at sixty miles an hour. Then she seemed to make up her mind.

'Roger, it's a bit complicated to explain.'

I'll bet it is, I thought.

'Try,' I encouraged. 'Keep it simple and I might understand it.'

She frowned. 'Please, Roger, I know it's difficult for you but believe me it's just as difficult for me. It would help me immensely if you would tell me all that has happened since you left Glasgow.'

Stalling, I wondered? Doesn't she know? Oh well, what is there to lose? If she knows already there's no harm in telling her — if she doesn't, then Leighton certainly knows and it cannot do his cause any good to tell her and it might do it some harm. And any course that could do that got my vote. So I gave Claire a blow-by-blow account of my activities since I received Johnny's letter the previous afternoon, omitting just one thing, my knowledge of what Johnny created.

116

Leighton knew about that, but I still believed that the fewer people who learned about it the better. So I edited that bit out. It was a longer story than I had anticipated and Claire kept asking questions to clarify points, so that we were approaching the outskirts of Paisley before I finished.

'I did think of trying to get a motor launch to take me back, rather than go on the *Glen Sannox,* but either I'd have to jimmy the ignition somehow and steal it — even supposing it had petrol in its tank — or try to find the owner — there's a problem in itself! — and persuade him to take me across the Firth. And somehow I didn't fancy trying to explain the situation to some law-abiding owner.'

Claire nodded. She had the Mini's side-lights on and we were passing the Coats memorial church on one side and the Paisley College of Technology on the other.

'Now,' I said, 'it's your turn.'

'Not quite, Roger. Just a few more questions. I take it Leighton has Dr. Marshall's letter now.'

'Yes.'

'Then really you have no proof of anything you've told me. No, no! I believe you, Roger, but would the police? Do you think they would believe in this fantastic story of a super-organisation called ISGAR? And if they interviewed Leighton and Cornelius and the others, do you think they'd give themselves away?'

A rhetorical question. Claire went on. 'You're sure Leighton doesn't have Dr. Marshall's papers or know where they are?'

'I'm sure.'

'And you don't know where they are?'

'Johnny must have over-estimated my intelligence.'

'Or was even cleverer than we've given him credit for.' She frowned. 'Try this problem, Roger. You believe you might be picked up and that so much pressure put on you (possibly by drugs) that you have to tell the truth. And yet you've so arranged it that the truth is still a lie. Your opponents can examine the contents of your mind and still not get what they're looking for. How do you do it?'

I thought about it for a time. It still didn't make sense.

'No, somehow I don't think it's quite like that. He surely knew that if they couldn't get the papers and prototype they could squeeze a new description out of him.'

'Y-yes. Which was what they would have done if he hadn't tried to escape and broken his neck.'

By accident — or on purpose? Was that what you did, Johnny? I suddenly felt tired and depressed, my aches tugging at the sleeve of my mind.

'Where are you taking me?'

'Not your flat,' she replied. 'Leighton undoubtedly will have telephoned to have someone waiting for you — on the off-chance that you did somehow slip across to the mainland. Probably inside the flat.' I had a sudden vision of a man sitting in the darkness of the lounge, waiting . . . listening for the sound of my key in the lock. 'And there may well be someone outside your Department. No. I'm taking you to Westbank Quadrant. You'd better stay the night with me. In the morning we can decide what to do next.'

I was tired of being pushed around like a cork tossed about on a fast-moving river, bashed off one rock on to another, but at this moment I realised how sensible the move was. After a night's sleep I felt I could better weigh up the situation. In particular I still had to solve the problem of Johnny's discovery and its hiding-place. Somewhere along the line I had mis-interpreted the letter he had sent me. I sighed.

'All right, I give in, I'll come quietly.' Roger the Lodger, I thought.

Her lips parted. 'Now let's give our undivided attention to the road. We're getting near home and although it's a very small chance that anyone will spot us I'd rather concentrate on that than satisfy your curiosity. Explanations later.'

It made sense. Thereafter we both kept quiet while the Mini roared through the bright-lit Clyde Tunnel, up Balshagray Avenue, cut across to Hyndland between grey and red sandstone tenements where Johnny and Laura had once had a flat then crossed Byres Road into Ashton Road, University Avenue and finally down the hill into Gibson Street. It was now quite dark. Claire pulled in to the side.

'Just as a precaution, Roger, you'd better get in the back. I shouldn't think for a moment that there's anyone waiting here but there's no sense in taking chances.'

118

I crouched down once more in the back of the van. A minute later we had drawn up in Westbank Quadrant in front of the close. Claire took the basket and a camera from the back and climbed the steps in front of the entrance. When she returned she loaded herself with some of the other things in the car, got out and made a show of re-arranging them. Fortunately the nearest street-lamp was a good fifty feet away and the steep riverbank of the Kelvin bordered one side of the narrow, curving street. Her whisper came to me.

'Now! There's no one about and no one at any of the windows.'

I limped up the steps into the close, Claire following me. Inside the flat she took off the blue windcheater, hung it on a wall peg, turned and inspected me, her head tilted a little. She grinned.

'You look a mess, Roger.' She felt the sleeve of my shirt. 'Your clothes are still damp. Wait here a minute.'

Swiftly she went through the door nearest the main door to return a half-minute later carrying an enormous white bath towel, a tin of Elastoplast dressings, a very feminine-looking housecoat and a small pale blue battery-operated razor.

'There's plenty of hot water. Go and soak while I make something to eat. You can wear the bath towel and housecoat while your clothes are drying.'

Wordlessly I took the things from her and entered the bathroom. As the bath filled, I stripped, noticing with a certain morbid satisfaction that I had been right about the blisters. There were five: the ones on my heels and on my left small toe had broken. I climbed into the bath and wallowed dazedly in the steaming water for a time before making an attempt to clean the brown peat-stains from my feet and hands. The open blisters stung like fury, as did the cut on my cheek when I washed my face.

Finally I dried myself, wiped the condensation from the mirror above the washhand basin and shaved the two-day bristly growth from my face. I thought several times the little cylindrical razor was going to pack it in but it struggled on, buzzing stubbornly. After Elastoplasting my feet I tried to solve the problem of the bath towel, finally wrapping it around me kilt-fashion. I draped the dainty housecoat about my shoulders. If I'd tried to put my arms through the sleeves I'd have ripped it. Catching a glimpse of myself in the mirror I murmured, 'All set for the camp fire, ducky?' Gathering up my discarded clothing, I left the bathroom.

'In the lounge, Roger.'

I entered the big front room and halted. Claire looked up from the long coffee table where she was arranging dishes. Her eyes twinkling, she nodded slowly.

'Dead kinky.' Her mouth twitched then she laughed outright. I grinned. At the same time I thought I detected strain in her laugh. I moved towards the fireplace. She recovered and pointed to the couch facing the fire.

'Sit down. You really look a lot better. If you put your clothes over there I'll arrange them in front of radiators later.'

She gave me coffee then sat down beside me.

'You must let me tell this in my own way, Roger. Afterwards you can ask all the questions you like.'

'All right.'

'Leighton told you only part of the truth about ISGAR. He said a group of powerful men founded it in the Edwardian era.' I nodded. 'This was a lie. ISGAR was founded about twenty-five years previously.'

'But that puts it back to — ' I broke off.

'Yes. To eighteen seventy-six, to be precise. But the group of men, scientists, statesmen, philosophers and scholars, who did found it, had motives very far removed from those of Leighton's crew. The wars that had shocked them were the American Civil War and the Franco-Prussian War, the first two modern wars to use railroads to carry troops and munitions, ironclads, submarines, Krupps breech-loading guns. We have to remember that more than a half million men died in the Civil War alone. Anyway, this group of men, some of whom at least were of the calibre of Galton, Darwin, Sidgwick and Kelvin, thought they could construct an international network of influential men of their persuasions that could work underground to curb the insanities or simple incompetencies of the world's rulers. ISGAR was originally the acronym of International Society for Guidance and Restraint.'

'And what methods did they plan to — sorry, Claire, I'm interrupting.'

'No, it's all right. They simply thought an international body of rational men, if organised and with a good communications network with powerful resources, could always thwart and nullify the forces that produce wars.'

It all sounded extraordinarily naive and unrealistic to me, rather like some of the alleged questions in old-time Cambridge Maths Tripos — 'In an apple-pie not more than thirty feet high . . .' I said as much to Claire. She nodded.

'It probably was. Yet the sober fact of the matter is that intelligent men of every nation can agree and be of absolutely one mind about the insanity of war. Nevertheless games theory computers state that there is only a twenty per cent chance of avoiding a major war before 2000 A.D.

'Anyway, almost from the beginning, there were members who argued that most of mankind were so irrational and stupid that appeals by politicians to their greed or prejudices or jingoism could always lead them by the nose into a war. And that the only solution was to employ any means behind the scenes to control events.

'The original members held out against this policy but the First World War with its staggering insanities came along and proved, at any rate to the advocates of force, that they were right. So they split off and formed ISGAR-2, the International Society for Guidance and Rule. This society is the one Leighton belongs to. I'm afraid the high ideals of the first ISGAR were quickly lost sight of — Lord Acton was so right! — and to the top people in ISGAR-2, the human race is simply a set of peasants to be exploited and controlled.'

'What happened to ISGAR-1?'

'It still exists — but it spends most of its time trying to combat ISGAR-2. And not very successfully. ISGAR-2 soon decided that if it was going to succeed, it had to destroy ISGAR-1, who knew of its existence.' She frowned. 'It almost succeeded, especially these past few years, even though our group adopted the tactics of illegal communist and resistance movements. But with this drug, it's easy to see how they can systematically winkle out our people.'

'Our group? Then you're — ?' Claire nodded.

'Yes, I'm a member of ISGAR-1. I have been for three years.' Her eyes searched mine. 'When we discovered the existence of Leighton's group at Carradale House some time ago we tried to get someone inside there. We finally succeeded though not to the level we would have liked.' A guest or a staff member? I wondered. 'When this business with Dr. Marshall arose, our man notified us of Dr. Marshall's death, also of the supreme importance Leighton attached to Marshall's work.'

'Was he able to learn the nature of Johnny's research?'

'No. All he could discover was that ISGAR-2 had put an absolutely top priority on the matter and that you were in some way the key to the problem.'

But the key didn't fit, I thought. I drank some coffee. 'Go on,' I invited. Claire refilled the cups while she spoke.

'Well, I went down to Arran to be on the spot. I had some vague idea that with our agent's help I might in some way gather more information about the reason why ISGAR-2 thought the matter so important. In addition we had taken other steps such as monitoring your mail. I'm sorry, Roger, but we had to do it.'

I said nothing but kept watching her face.

'Then you arrived. At first I wondered if you had come down because you had received Dr. Marshall's letter, but as you know, I soon learned you were still in the dark.'

Oh yes, Gullible's Travels in person.

'Our agent's work at Carradale House took him out of the way at the crucial time and he did not learn that you had gone there last night, or had spent the night there until after you had been taken to the Doon and escaped.' She laughed shakily, a look of distress in her eyes. 'Believe me, Roger, it's only in books or films that the spy inside the organisation always manages to be around at the crucial moments. But he did contrive to get away and phone me to tell me that you were on the run, had ditched your car at Monyquil Farm and were somewhere up in the hills. I thought that the best thing I could do was to come down by the first available boat in the hope that I could do something. I knew you'd try to get off the island and that probably Leighton would have picketed the pier so I finally decided to remain in the vicinity around sailing-times. Our man elected to stay at Carradale House in case they brought you back there.

'Oh Roger,' she gasped, 'I've never spent such a hellish time in my life as I did waiting at that pier. I could have taken the wrong decision; I knew that if Leighton himself came along he'd suspect immediately. While I sat there doing nothing, I kept picturing you being hunted across the hills above Monyquil.' Her hand touched mine. It was cold and trembled a little and I saw that her eyes glistened with tears. 'I could have passed out in relief when your unshaven mug appeared above the wall.'

I pressed her hand.

'I wasn't exactly sorry to see you, Claire. Thank you very much for being there.' I scanned her face. Surely I wasn't deluding myself in thinking her concern genuine and personal and not merely due to the fact that somewhere in the three pounds of protoplasm I called a brain, knowledge of Johnny's hiding-place lay hidden. Abruptly there swept over me that tingling, exciting, almost stomach-unsettling feeling of high alertness experienced before the first-ever dive off the high springboard, or the first youthful attempt to kiss a girl, or the first time you pilot a plane solo.

'Claire — ' I whispered and with no conscious decision taken I found myself moving forward. She leaned towards me and my lips met hers. I was aware of many things, my left arm about her shoulders, the rough fabric texture of the settee back pressing on one side of it, the warmth of her on the other, the fragrance of her dark hair, the soft pressure of her body against mine, our knees touching, the warm sweetness of her mouth, all that I had dreamed it would be. She half-closed her eyes and then opened them. Reluctantly I drew away. She looked at me, her lips still parted, her breath rapid.

'I love you, Claire. I hadn't meant to tell you so soon. In fact, I've wondered if I could ever steel myself to tell you. I suppose I felt that it might mean the end of our — ' She put her left hand over my mouth and shook her head. Smiling, she took her hand away, bent forward and kissed me then relaxed into my arms again. At the end of the kiss she looked at me, her eyes troubled.

'I must tell you something, Roger. It was quite by chance that I met you that afternoon on the Moor. But when I learned who you were, I looked upon our meeting as a stroke of luck and so — '

123

'So you invited yourself to dinner with me.'

'Yes. But then, Roger, I found my interest growing, especially after the drive we made that evening round the island. And ever since then, my dear, I've been hoping that your feelings were growing as fast as mine.' She smiled. 'I rather thought they had but you seemed terribly ...... wary?'

Yes, I thought, a leetle gunshy. In the midst of my exuberant elation, it came home to me how for years I had deliberately avoided any deep emotional involvement with the few women I'd taken about, how I'd sidestepped the matchmaking attempts of friends. But now. . .

'Sometime I'll tell you about that, Claire. The main point now is that I love you.' I shook my head in frustration. 'I wish I could coin new words, mint-fresh and sparkling and capable of describing just how I feel about you.' A recollection, almost an echo, of having thought much the same thing about the inadequacy of words in other circumstances came to me — yes, my first phone-call to Laura after Johnny's death — and then, with all the shock effect of a blow in the stomach, my subconscious used the bridge to tell me where Johnny had hidden his work. My face must have given me away.

'What's wrong, Roger?'

I swallowed. 'I know where Johnny's papers are.'

'What? How — ?'

I hurriedly waved her to silence as I tried to recall Johnny's exact words on the tape-recording. Leighton had asked where Johnny had hidden the things and Johnny had replied: 'In the ground.' And in answer to Leighton's next question, he had said he had buried them *under* the slaughter stone circle, not *in* or *within* as one might have expected considering that the circle was about fifty feet in diameter. Leighton had confirmed that the slaughter stone circle was one of the Tormore Circles and then he had asked:

'Is your work buried under the slaughter stone?'

And Johnny, unable to do anything else, had spoken the literal truth when he said 'Yes'.

But what Leighton didn't know — at least I hoped to God he didn't — was that in the acre of garden at Boquhan, Johnny had laid out a scale model of the Tormore system, on which scale the slaughter stone circle was just about one foot broad. And Laura had told me that he had been gone from bed for an hour or so the night he completed his work.

'Claire, did your people burgle Johnny's workshop?'

'Why yes. We hoped to find out what he was working on.'

Which was as I had suspected. Leighton's people, confident that they could get what they wanted from me, would probably not have bothered — at least, not yet. Claire, tensely curious, stared at me and I made up my mind.

'We've got to get moving again.' I told her my conclusions and she nodded. Standing up I retrieved my clothes. I grinned ruefully.

'For a number of reasons, least of which is a reluctance to put on these damp clothes and exercise my blistered feet, I'd have preferred staying here.'

She grinned. 'I know, it's a pity, but dooty is dooty. I'll get a torch and my windcheater while you dress. You'd better bring that coal shovel as well.'

I drew on the slightly clammy garments as fast as I could, switched off radiator and lights and entered the hall. We left the flat and went downstairs. Glancing at my watch I saw it was just approaching ten-thirty. As far as we could see there were no watchers or unknown cars about. I got into the Minivan beside Claire and she took it round the far end of Westbank Quadrant from Gibson Street into Otago Street. It was cloudy and really dark. Several times I found myself gazing at Claire's profile and wondering in bemused bewilderment, like so many men in similar circumstances, what on earth she could see in me that attracted her. Then I gazed ahead through the windscreen at the silver ribbon of road and the gleaming cats'-eyes rushing towards us like tracer bullets.

We reached Boquhan about eleven-ten. While Claire sat in the van, I tried to phone Laura from the public call-box. There was no reply and I remembered she had talked about closing up the house and going to stay with her mother. I replaced the receiver and got back in the van. We parked it under some trees off the narrow side-road leading into the little settlement, cut round through a field that bordered the foot of Johnny's garden and approached warily. In the darkness we listened

125

for at least ten minutes, judging by that time that any watcher would have given himself away by a change in position. I squeezed Claire's arm and we climbed the wire fence.

The dozen or so houses had been scattered irregularly over the area, care being taken to leave as many clumps of trees and rhododendron bushes intact as possible. In addition, Johnny's home was on the periphery, his garden sloping downwards to the field we had come across. It was on a flat lawn at the foot of the slope, bordered by shrubs, that he had laid out his model of the Tormore Circles, adding to it from time to time the latest circles and outliers he had plotted. Its situation was therefore so secluded that we could risk a few blinks from the heavily dimmed-out torch to orientate ourselves.

I knelt down. The small circle of stones looked intact. With the shovel I skimmed off the four inches of turf inside the stones to lay bare the square concrete slab on to which Johnny had cemented the stones. Gripping the rough edge I heaved it up and out. Dark, moist earth lay underneath. I dug into it. Surely I was right this time. Six inches below the surface, my shovel struck something that yielded.

'Shine the torch in here,' I whispered. Claire held the torch in the hole. In the pool of light I saw a packet about the size of a paper-back novel, wrapped in sacking, lying on top of a larger package, also covered in sacking. I felt myself sweating. The fruit of the tree of knowledge. I glanced once at the strained dimly-illuminated face of my companion as I scooped the small packet out of the hole and handed it to her. The bigger package was a good fifty pounds in weight, muscle-wrenching in its awkwardness to lift out. Dragging it aside, I made sure that the hole contained nothing else then scraped as much of the earth as possible into it. I replaced the slab and patted down the turf. Getting up, with the heavy package in my arms, I breathed: 'Let's get out of here fast.'

On the journey back we neither spoke nor attempted to open the packages, as if by mutual agreement. Once in the flat, we entered the lounge; Claire switched both bars of the radiator on and shrugged out of her windcheater. As I placed the packages on the long coffee table, she asked:

'What about your clothes, Roger?'

'They'll do, Claire. In fact they're almost dry now. Have you scissors?'

I snipped the thread from both packages and stripped off the coarse sacking, the smells of earth and damp canvas reaching my nostrils. Next came several layers of polythene. The smaller package, as I had suspected, contained closely-written papers.

'Johnny's handwriting,' I muttered.

The object in the larger package looked like an amateurish attempt to construct a portable television set with a ten-inch screen though if that were so there were far too many knobs and dials on the unpainted front and sides. Coiled round it was about eight feet of flex ending in — Oh God, I thought, an ordinary thirteen-amp square pin plug. I bit my lip and picked up the papers. One glance at the summary on the first page was enough.

Claire turned to face me. Her eyes reflected the fear in mine.

'What is it, Roger?'

I nodded at the innocent-looking box on the table.

'If Johnny really succeeded — and I have no doubts that he did — that is a timescope — a device for looking into the past.'

9   The Fruit of the Tree of Knowledge

Claire stared at me, her eyes wide.

'A timescope. Do you seriously mean — ? But is it possible?'

'Yes. It's certainly possible in principle. No paradox involved. You can't alter the past or visit it — too many paradoxes there — but there's no reason in principle why you can't view it. In a sense an astronomer does it when he looks at a distant galaxy.'

'And this is what Leighton was after.' Her features registered complete bafflement. 'But . . . even if it does what you say, Roger, why should ISGAR-2 attach so much importance to getting it? They're not interested in historical research.'

I felt numb and tired.

'Let me read this, Claire. While I'm doing so, ask yourself the question: how do you define the past, the present and the future? In particular, when does the present become the past?'

I began to read. It was tough going and there were sections in tensor calculus, proofs of lemmas and theorems, that I simply accepted on trust. It seemed that Johnny had been puzzled by some results we'd been getting in our measurements of the recently-discovered three degree background radiation. He finally linked the anomalous energy component present to certain implications in the Benezra-Tsien Unified Field Theory and drew conclusions from it that I interpreted hesitantly as saying that at every point in the space-time continuum there existed information about every other point no matter how 'distant'. According to Johnny, the wave particles he was talking about — he called them 'chronons' — had a time component and were propagated by all matter during its material existence. And just as a radio receiver could be designed and built to collect and amplify certain wavelengths, so a timescope could be constructed at any space-time point to filter out from the total information at that point the signal or set of 'chronons' from some other selected space-time point. In fact his first timescope was a modification of the Department three degree radiation monitor. The results he got with it so astounded him that he quickly restored it to 'normal' and continued his work in secret at Boquhan.

He then used the Unified Field Theory to demonstrate that in our particular universe, because of the asymmetry of time, timescanning (the name he gave to the process of using a timescope) was possible only from future to past and not from past to future. I simply couldn't follow this last part of his argument — even if I'd been fresher I doubt if the sheets of symbolic logic would have meant much to me — but I accepted his thesis gratefully for I didn't think I could have lived with the possibility of seeing the future as well as the past.

And then in the last section of this staggering achievement he described a simple timescope, capable of being constructed out of standard off-shelf electronic components and working off the normal household 250 volt supply, with a range of eighty mile-years. There was evidently some sort of trade-off between distance and time elapsed. He also gave graphs of theoretical performance against power that indicated millenia ranges of time to be available with quite moderate loads.

When I put down the papers my hands trembled. I looked at Claire. Her face was stricken.

'No secrets,' she whispered. 'Is that it, Roger?'

I nodded, 'A little part of it.' She was terribly quick on the uptake, I thought, though of course she knew that if Leighton was after it, it had to be far from being a simple tool for academic research.

I summarised Johnny's paper. Her eyes luminous in her chalk-white face, she gazed at the squat plywood box sitting doucely on the coffee-table. Now that I understood the design, the controls made sense. There was an on-off switch, a three-inch circular protractor on top, accurate to about a degree, to act as a kind of compass-rose; a set of circular time scales and a set of distance scales. The time scales were calibrated in tens of miles, miles, tenths of a mile and yards. Another distance scale read in tens of yards and yards and was labelled 'High-Low.' A small lever had an angular scale beside it labelled 'Pitch-Yaw.' With these controls and a large scale map, it would be possible to 'land' in the vicinity of a town, say, and then home in to a particular place inside the town using a map of the town. This simple procedure was possible because the design of the timescope allowed for the twisting of the geodesics. I supposed that in a longer range model a full-sized third dimensional distance scale would be required to allow for the curvature of the Earth.

'We'll have to try it,' I pointed out. With obvious reluctance, Claire nodded. I unwound the flex. While she was plugging it in, I made sure all the dials were zeroed. Claire came back and sat beside me.

'Supposing I set it for exactly sixty years ago in this room?' I suggested tentatively.

'All right.' She followed my movements as I switched on and turned the decade dial. The screen flickered and lit up. The eeriest sensation I have ever experienced enveloped me coldly as I gazed at a clear black-and-white view of a large room fitted with the solid, cluttered, antimacassar furniture of a bygone era, gas-mantled ceiling lights in a cylindrical pleated shade, heavy, tasselled window curtains, horse-

129

hair chairs flanking a massive mahogany sideboard supporting huddled ornaments and a bowl of glistening wax fruit, ugly, dark, embossed wall-paper to waist height topped by a soup-plate sized flower pattern. It seemed to be late afternoon, almost five o'clock according to the clock in the middle of the cluttered mantelpiece. There was no movement in that room we had snatched out of limbo, none at least for the half-minute we sat there hypnotised before I stretched out a hand to alter the time-scale. Before I could touch it, I froze. The clock was chiming, its mellifluous tones reaching us across six decades of history.

Claire's gasp was almost a sob. 'Sound, as well.'

The door in that room — this room? — opened. A maid entered, black dress, white apron, mob cap, a burning taper in her hand. She crossed to the already prepared fire and lit it. Straightening up, she rested one hand on the mantelpiece while she waited to make sure the fire had really caught.

'For the master coming home from business,' Claire whispered in horror, almost as if the girl could hear her. We watched her leave the room. The fire began to crackle hospitably. This time I switched off.

Is this how ghosts feel, I wondered, when they look on at life but are unable to influence it? I took a deep breath.

'Once more,' I said quietly. 'The outbreak of the last war. Botanic Gardens.'

I made a rough estimate of direction and distance from Westbank Quadrant, reset the dials, also the time scales for September 3rd, 1939, as closely as I could. We landed within the glass walls of the Kibble Palace. From the pale light and shadows cast by palm trees and other semi-tropical vegetation, I judged it to be early evening. I verniered the position to the gates of the Botanic Gardens, where the Sunday newspaper sellers stood. There was nothing to be seen. Very slowly I turned the thick perspex day-dial. Two intervals ahead we found it. A bright Sunday morning with dark headlines, 'Germans Invade Poland,' and well-dressed people buying papers, the women in page-boy hair-styles and square-shouldered costumes, the men in oddly wide-brimmed hats and suits that didn't differ so markedly from modern conservative male attire. Box-like Austin Sevens, Hillmans with sharp bonnets and hardly any boot passed, tram cars trundled across the Botanic Gardens points or turned down Byres Road, their metal tyres drawing squeals from the tracks. The peal of bells from the tall grey pointed steeple of the church opposite the entrance to the Botanic Gardens called the Hillhead district to morning service. Ten minutes later Britain at a million radio sets would hear the tired voice of Neville Chamberlain announce that a state of war now existed between Great Britain and Germany.

I switched off and turned to Claire.

'As the adverts say: "opens up a new era".'

'It's terrifying, Roger.'

'It's fascinating, too.' Quite consciously I was testing her appreciation of the timescope's potentialities. 'Just think what a powerful lot one could do for historical research. The thousand riddles of history solved by simple inspection. What price *Through A Glass Darkly* now? You could write the sequel *"But Then Face to Face"*.'

She looked at me. There was no gainsaying what I had said. All of history was laid bare to the historians using a powerful enough timescope. Perhaps even the origins of man himself. Was Richard III the original wicked uncle? Tune in to the late fifteenth century and find out. What were the real reasons for the fall of the Roman Empire? Spend two or three years actually watching then write a really definitive thesis for your doctorate — none of the usual literary transfer of bones from one graveyard to another; these bones could be clothed with flesh and resurrected to act out their lives and passions, their joys and miseries. Of course it was not as simple as that. To investigate a particular historical sequence long searches would be required, persons would have to be backtracked to obtain leads to other relevant actors; interpretations and judgements of their words and deeds would have to be made but the record, complete, unalterable, with all the warts put in, would be accessible.

Claire said as much. I nodded.

'And modern history, say of the past twenty years? Remember, no secrets.'

'Yes, no secrets. How the politicians would loathe and hate and fear this. All their platitudes and evasions and downright lies spotlighted

131

immediately they spoke.' She shook her head. 'This is where it all begins to look frightening. Supposing a timescope took its place beside the TV and radio sets in every household. It doesn't look too difficult to build.' ~

'It isn't. That's one of the most terrifying things about it. A competent electronics engineer could construct one in three hours from off-shelf components. It's like television or radar. The big step was conceiving the idea and formulating the theory.'

'So it could be mass-produced. Newspaper and TV reporters could take one to the scene of any event and re-run that event. Or people with timescopes that included that space-time point could view it for themselves. No fictitious frontier incidents, every aggressor spotlighted in the act.'

'The police would love this.'

'Indeed they would. You simply re-run the crime and catch the criminal by following him on the timescope. I suppose conviction in court would automatically follow when a timescope re-enactment was viewed by the jury.'

'Do you then think timescanning should be available to everyone, not just operated by the government?'

'Yes. It is perfectly obvious it would be the ultimate weapon in a police state's control of its people. Roger! It makes Orwell's Big Brother completely passe. And if any Intelligence Service had it, they'd have access to everyone's secrets.'

'And the possibilities for blackmail. How many influential or wealthy men have episodes in their lives they'd do practically anything to keep hidden, even in these tolerant times. Quite a few, I imagine.'

Claire sat silently, thoughtfully. 'If we agree that no group should possess the timescope, are we sure the other situation, where it is available to everyone, is not as bad?'

'It gives people the truth about events.'

'But can people stand the truth? Oh yes, Roger, about many things, minor and even major things, they can. And about world events they deserve the truth. Most of the miseries of the past sixty years have come about because people weren't given the truth but were fed a pack of lies. But could a man survive the knowledge that his life was an open

132

book to his fellows, to his nearest and dearest, that any deceit he contemplated was sure to be found out, with only the trivial, minor hypocrisies of good-manners available to him?' She paused. 'That from cradle to the grave he had to assume an invisible TV camera was following him about.'

'Thou, God, seeest me.'

'Oh no, Roger, it's worse, much worse than that. Whatever our religious beliefs may be, we have always been comforted by the knowledge that whatever God saw, he wouldn't tell.'

'Would it be as bad as that?' I asked. 'Would people, ordinary decent people, take a delight in spying on their fellows?'

'I don't know, Roger. The detective agencies do quite well; thousands of couples in our western civilisation live in a state of bitter, gnawing suspicion. I don't know.'

'And if they did see their fellows as less than perfect,' I murmured, 'would they really learn something new? — would they not simply make allowances, knowing their own imperfections?'

'Oh, Roger, I wish I could think so.'

I shrugged. 'Maybe I'm being too soft-hearted and soft-headed. The timescope certainly offers the sick element in our society an inexhaustible supply of stimuli. You want a few kicks? Tune in to the dungeons of the Holy Inquisition or to Dachau or Buchenwald any time between the late thirties and 1945.' I felt myself sighing. 'Yes, when you come right down to it, there are thousands who'd settle down with beer and crisps in front of the screen for an evening's entertainment. Just like the telly. But real!'

'I'm afraid so, Roger. At its mildest, the old gossip who now spends her day peering at her neighbours through the curtains will pry on their activities with the timescope.' She shivered, her face tight and bleak. 'No privacy. Quite literally, no privacy.' She bit her lip. 'On another plane, Roger, what about religion? Do people want the truth there?'

'"What is truth, asking jesting Pilate, and stayed not for an answer".'

'I don't know what the truth is,' said Claire, 'but timescanning may well throw light on the origins of most of the major religions, not to mention the minor ones.'

I thought of all the multifarious branches of the millenia-old Christian church (how these Christians love one another); the followers of Mohammed and Buddha; the variegated gods of India. What would remain, I wondered, if under the laser-beam of the timescope the age-old encrustations of legend melted and vanished into mist? But the scholars had refused to look through Galileo's telescope — the fossils found in rock strata were obviously tests of our faith, put there that Sunday morning, October 23rd, 4004 B.C. when the Earth was created. And I, thundered Wilberforce, put man on the side of the angels, not apes.

Eppur, si muove — and yet it moves. It takes time, I thought, but with patience and enough push, each new step is finally established and accepted. The content of my thought made me look at my watch. One-thirty a.m.

'Twenty-four hours ago,' I said, 'I was in a cellar in Carradale House. Now I am here after a not uneventful day. We have the timescope. Let that be sufficient. Neither of us is in a fit state to assess what our course of action should be.' I got to my feet, knowing that I would be stiff when I woke up. Claire rose. I took her in my arms and smiled at her.

'A successful day, Miss Stewart. Acquisitions: life, liberty and the pursuit of happiness; one timescope, weight fifty-five pounds, one girl, weight — ?'

Her eyes sparkled. 'Never you mind.' She kissed me and I held her close.

'Now,' she said in business-like tones, 'a place for you to sleep.' She sketched despair on her face. 'I simply do not see you in baby-doll pyjamas. You will have to sleep as nature intended.'

'Yes, please.'

'And you will doubtless be overjoyed to learn that there is a comfortable bed in the guest room where you can get a good night's sleep.'

'Ha, ha!' I said dolefully. She leaned back and regarded me solemnly.

'Only one thing counts with me just now, Roger; to smash ISGAR-2. Once that is done,' her dark eyelashes swept once over her blue eyes,

134

'we can thing of other things . . . like this!' And bringing her hands up to my cheeks she kissed me lingeringly, the warm pressure of her parted lips at once a relevation and a pledge. In a daze of emotion, I saw her tilt her head back. 'There!' she said, her twinkling eyes scanning my face as if assessing the result. Before I knew it, she was out of my arms and out of the door. I found myself gazing at the fire and grinning like a loon.

I became conscious that someone was shaking me, that I had a wide variety of aches and that a voice was urging me to wake up. I surfaced, turned over from my side to my back and opened my eyes. Claire bent over me. When my eyes met hers, she smiled and poked a stiff forefinger into my shoulder muscle. I registered agony.

'Wake up, layabout. Breakfast will be ready in ten minutes.'

I sat up and modestly tucked the bedclothes round my waist, noticing with amusement that far from wearing baby-doll gear, she had on sensible pyjamas under a short, patterned pale-blue and white housecoat. Even to my bleary eye she looked remarkably attractive.

'What's the time?'

'Eight forty-five. I managed to get most of the dried mud brushed out of your clothes and I've sewn up the rips in the trousers but I'm afraid their best days are over.' I rotated my shoulders gingerly and thought: and their owner.

Over orange juice, eggs and bacon, toast and coffee in the kitchen, we tried to agree on a course of action. From my point of view the situation was far from simple. Quite apart from my feelings for the girl sitting opposite me in our delightfully domestic tableau, I had to weigh up the possible consequences if (a) I donated the timescope to Claire's group to help them win their struggle against ISGAR-2, (b) destroyed it as too dangerous to let loose, (c) turned it over to the authorities. And with respect to course (c), one had to ask, which authorities? In addition, I had hanging over me the knowledge that it was open season on Roger Arnott. Claire herself couldn't see any course that quite definitely led the field, having little or no potentially dangerous consequences through she tended to favour arming her group.

'Frankly, Roger, we're being beaten in our fight with ISGAR-2. With their resources, we're finding it difficult to survive, let alone nullify their operations. But with the timescope we'd be able to trace every cell and ramification in their structure, learn all their secrets and be in a position to give law enforcement agencies the world over all the information necessary to wind up ISGAR-2.'

She read doubt in my face.

'Surely it would mean the end of ISGAR-2?' she persisted.

'It certainly would. But it would again mean that a group of people had a monopoly of the timescope. I'm sorry, Claire, I just can't make my mind up at the moment. I've got to have more time to think.'

She rose. 'Time's running out, Roger. In a war there's always a deadline on decisions, whether or not you've got enough information to decide sensibly.' She glanced at the electric wall-clock. 'Look, darling, I've got to make two phone calls, one to Benson (he's our agent at Carradale House), the other, well, higher up.'

I stood up. 'Isn't that a bit dangerous? — I mean, the first call.'

She shook her head. 'We make these check-calls at definite intervals and at pre-arranged times, from certain public phone-boxes. It's as near as we can come to a fail-safe procedure. Failure to make the call or failure to include certain phrases lets the others know something has gone wrong.' She went to the door. 'Now I must go and dress, Roger. The first call is from Benson at 9.15 and I have to go down to Byres Road for it. The second one I make at 9.25. I'll be back by 9.45.'

I suddenly remembered that somehow Leighton had nobbled the telephone system in Arran. Claire bit her lip.

'It may have been repaired by now. While I'm dressing, check for me. Telephone's in the sitting room.'

By the time she rejoined me, I was able to tell her that the G.P.O. engineers had been on the ball and restored communications. She was wearing a roll-necked sweater, the blue windcheater and ski-pants and when she laughed in relief, a sudden stab of fear hit me. I gripped her upper arms and shook her gently.

'Be careful, Claire. It'd be an awful nuisance to have to find another girl to take to that concert.'

We kissed once then she left. I shut the main door, conscious that I had deliberately avoided asking her if she meant to tell her superiors about the timescope. Aware also that I was now forced to a decision, I returned to the lounge. Ten nail-biting minutes later I had made up my mind. I fetched a quarto sheet of typing paper from Claire's workroom, sat down on the couch again and began to write.

'Dear Claire,

 I'm sorry to duck out like this, especially after all you've done for me but I must have time to think. I'm going to find some place, a hotel or boarding house to hole up in while I decide what to do. I shall choose a course of action by six p.m. tomorrow night and will phone you here at that time to let you know. My belief is that to consider the problem for any longer time is unlikely to bring me to any wiser decision.

   Believe me, Claire, I love you.

     Roger.'

I read it over, wondered if I should have signed it 'Hamlet' instead, propped it up against a vase on the coffee table where she'd be sure to see it, and phoned the Botanic Gardens taxi rank. Retrieving the sacking Johnny had used, I quickly parcelled up the timescope, including the papers. I carried the package into the hall, placed it just inside the main door and returned to the oriel window to look out for the taxi. The time by my watch was 9.24. There was still no sign of the cab. I bit my lip. Three storeys down, the narrow street was empty but for two parked cars, one of them Claire's Minivan. She must have taken the Mini Cooper, I thought. Beyond the railing on the other side of the Quadrant, the vertical embankment fell to the sludge-laden waters of the Kelvin, bounded by stone walls or dank, unhealthy-looking vegetation. Where the hell was that taxi?

I felt myself stiffen. Not a taxi but a Mini Cooper swerved into Westbank Quadrant from Gibson Street and ripped along. Before I could move, its brakes screeched as it decelerated. I glanced back. A black Rover 2000 had entered the street at the other end and pulled across to block the Mini Cooper. The Mini Cooper tried to turn. Even for the Mini it was a tricky manoeuvre in the narrow road. It had to be a three-point turn; the driver carried it out at top speed with faultless gear-changing but to no avail. A third car, a 66 Zodiac, swept into the

Quadrant from Gibson Street and forced the Mini to stop to avoid a head-on collision.

Simultaneously, three men leapt from the Zodiac as Claire swung herself out of the Mini. She hesitated, looked back and saw three more men run from the Rover 2000. The first three grabbed her, lifted her and rushed her back to the Zodiac. They bundled her inside; one of the second trio poked his head inside the Mini as if searching for something. The other two waited. A man left the Zodiac and called out something. He handed a key over to one of the two waiting men, talked again, pointed to the Zodiac, waved his arm northwards and ran back to the Zodiac. He got in. Two seconds later, the big car, its engine howling, reversed rapidly along the Quadrant to Gibson Street, hesitated, backed out and was away. The remaining trio began to run towards the entrance three storeys below me.

The whole action couldn't have taken more than twenty-five seconds in which time I could not move a muscle though my brain worked in a horrified, unbelieving fashion, commenting on and explaining the sequence. Benson must have been careless last night; Claire came back at top speed to get me and the timescope away but Leighton must have drugged enough information from Benson to put some of ISGAR-2's mainland men on to us. They've got Claire's house key and they're coming up to collect me. I whirled, caught sight of the letter I had left Claire and sprinted for the hall. Picking up the package, I opened the main door as quietly as possible. The echoing clatter of feet two storeys down hit my ears. Breathing quickly, I forced myself to close the door with no sound but the click of the Yale before tiptoeing up the fourth flight of steps. I had just reached the landing above when the three men pounded up the remaining stairs. Heavy breathing came to my ears, then,

'This is it! C. Stewart.'

The rasping sound of the key being slipped into the lock was followed by the dull reverberation of the door being thrown back. I stood, panting, rage and fear chilling me, straining my ears to catch what was going on. Once or twice I head confused sounds. The sounds rose in volume and I stiffened, my nails biting into the palms of my hands.

'Shouldn't one of us stay at least to go over the flat?'

'No, some nosey parker may have seen the snatch and phoned the cops. Anyway, you saw the letter — he's scappa'ed. We'll come back tomorrow to get his phone call.'

'Okay, let's get out of here fast.'

The door closed, their feet clattered down the flights of stairs and silence filled the stairwell. I crept down to the third landing. As I reached the glass-panelled door dismay pushed aside other emotions. I had no key. Placing the weighty timescope on the rough brown mat, I rummaged in the ragbag of my mind for anything useful. Breaking the thick glass would create a crash that would bring out every soul in the close and I had no time to squander on elaborate explanations to highly sceptical neighbours.

I looked at the lock. It was a simple Yale. I pulled my wallet from my hip-pocket, opened it and tore out the rectangular, transparent plastic sheet that faced the card bearing my name and address and other particulars. I prayed fervently that it was flexible enough but not too flexible. Inserting it between door-jamb and door at the height of the Yale, I manoeuvred it, continually curbing my impatience every time it stuck. Black incubi of thoughts about neighbours appearing, or police, or Leighton's men, of Claire in their hands, of the need to hurry, gripped my shoulders as I worked. Quite suddenly, I felt the plastic give as it bent to slide round between the door-edge and the door. It stuck again, against the curved tongue of the lock and in a muck-sweat, I pressed it forward. The tongue sank back into the lock and the door swung open.

From the sitting-room window I saw that the Rover 2000 had gone though the Mini Cooper still stood by the kerb. A sense of fearful urgency driving me, I ripped the sacking off the timescope, noticing as I did so that the letter I had written Claire was gone. A sick, vicious rage welled up in me as I plugged in the timescope. Straightening up, I extracted a copy of the *Oxford Atlas* from Claire's bookshelves and returned to the couch. Opening the dark-blue volume, I found the map of Scotland. As far as I could judge, Carradale House at Tormore was

139

almost exactly thirty miles away, about twenty degrees south west of my present location. I set the dials to the required readings, including a present-time setting, and switched on.

The dull bluish screen lit up and I saw that I was over the sea, as if I hovered more than eighty feet above the greasily surging waves. With a forefinger on the orientation dial, I swung the timescope's field and found the coast a fifth of a mile away. I recognised immediately the Machrie village hall and golflinks. With shaking fingers I tracked in and swept up the coast to the entrance to Tormore Glen. Half a minute later I was exploring Carradale House room by room, floor by floor.

I had no success until I remembered the basement and the cellar I had been imprisoned in. At that level I moved along a corridor, through a steel door and into a large brightly-lit room. It was quite obviously a communications and data-storing centre, judging by the metal handy-angle shelves carrying row upon row of labelled files, the bank of filing cabinets, the powerful transmitter and receiver (I wondered if it was Leighton who was licenced as a ham radio operator as cover for the aerials), and the desks. A radio operator was seated before the control panel; two other men in shirtsleeves were busy in other parts of the room. And Leighton was present. He stood behind his desk, one hand rapping a pencil on the palm of the other, his face bearing the expression of a man in a quandary.

I pulled the phone towards me and dialled 100. While I waited for the operator to give me the number of Carradale House I tried to convince myself I held the trump card. I was still unconvinced by the time she found it.

10   Deadlight

Again I listened for an eternity. I heard the Glasgow operator ask Brodick for the number and the local operator's fainter reply. The burr-burr note was finally broken.

'Carradale House.'

I thought I recognised the voice. 'Miss Welsh?'

'Yes. Can I help you?'

' I want to speak to Mr. Leighton.'

'I'm sorry. I'm very much afraid Mr. Leighton is not available. Can I take a message?'

'Look. I know damn well he is there. Tell him Dr. Roger Arnott wants to speak to him.'

'Really, I do not see what right you have to adopt that tone — .' The bland tones were now one hundred proof vinegar and vitriol.

'Miss Welsh, this is quite literally a matter of life and death. Every moment counts. I know Mr. Leighton is in the house. If you do not get him you'll have someone's death on your conscience — and be out of a job.'

I heard her gasp and gobble. Then she breathed heavily. 'All right, Dr. Arnott. I shall try to find Mr. Leighton.' Each word should have corroded the diaphragm out of the phone.

I endured the next thirty seconds of silence. Cut off while Miss Welsh spoke on the extension system, I kept my eyes fixed on the timescope screen. No one seemed to be contacting Leighton. I was beginning to think in a savage fury that Cerberus was giving me the 'Sorry I searched but he's not to be found' routine when there was a click and a warm feminine voice spoke softly.

'Why, Dr. Arnott, how very nice to hear from you again.'

I expelled my breath. 'I want to speak to Leighton.'

141

Miss Cornelius paused. 'Of course. I'm sure he'll want to have a word with you. Would you like to hold on while I get him on the other extension?'

In the interval before she appeared on the screen I thought frenziedly, testing and discarding ideas. Then my attention was held fully once again. Leighton's startled expression was followed by his striding to the desk. He picked up the phone. Miss Cornelius left the room — to keep Miss Welsh busy, I wondered.

'Well, Arnott, I hardly thought I'd be speaking to you so soon after our recent encounter. May I congratulate you on your evasive powers?'

'Never mind that. I know your men have got Miss Stewart.'

His eyes narrowed slightly. 'Indeed?' He glanced at the communications operator's back.

'Where are they taking her?'

'Now really, Arnott, you can't expect me to answer that. Except to say that it'll be some place where we can play Twenty Questions with her.'

I relaxed a little. As I had hoped, they would keep her alive at least until they had extracted everything she knew about ISGAR-1. After that — I felt a suffocating desire to hurt him.

'Leighton, I think you had better listen carefully to what I have to say.'

With his free hand he rubbed his moustache thoughtfully, very sure of himself but obviously a little puzzled and curious.

'Go on.'

'You are seated at a desk in a basement room at Carradale House. In front of you is a short-wave radio with which you can contact your men. There are three men with you.'

This time he was visibly shocked; he stiffened and his eyes widened. His lips parted as he took a deep breath. Stretching out his left hand, he pressed a bell-push.

'You have just stretched out your left hand and pressed a bell-push. It lies four inches beyond the black intercom box with six switches. Your left hand is now gripping the edge of the desk.'

In the screen his face went a muddy grey colour and his forehead

142

glistened. His gaze wandered about in random fashion without direction. And then he began to get a grip on himself. I suppose no more than seven seconds of silence elapsed before he spoke. As he did so, Monty entered the scene and was waved to silence.

'You found it.' It was no question but a statement.

'Yes.'

'But I don't see how — .' There was almost a plaintive note in his voice.

'It's a long story and it'll keep.'

'What do you want, Arnott?' The question was asked in a hard, bargaining tone. He was far more resilient than I had given him credit for.

'I want Miss Stewart released.'

'Or else?'

'Or else I'll turn the timescope over to the authorities with a full account of the events leading to Johnny's death. I will then suggest that they *view* those events — and beyond.'

He thought furiously. Monty watched his face, trying to make sense of the one side of the conversation he could hear.

'And if I do release Miss Stewart?'

'Both she and I will disappear. ISGAR-1 will see to that. Before we go, I will destroy the model I am using now — the only model in existence — and also Dr. Marshall's papers. I should point out that quite deliberately I have not studied them in detail, in particular the part that gives circuit diagrams of the timescope so that even if you ultimately found me, you could not recover from me the ability to build another.'

'Why should you destroy your colleague's work?'

'Because I believe the human race isn't ready for it.'

'Yet you'd give it to the authorities if Miss Stewart wasn't released.'

'Like a shot.'

He compressed his lips and his eyes glinted up at Monty, standing beside him. I pressed on, unease growing within me.

'But I promise you I'll destroy everything as soon as I'm sure we're safe.'

He stood up, seemed about to lay down the phone, then asked: 'Can you hear me through the 'scope?'

'Yes.'

He set the phone down beside its cradle and walked across to the operator.

'Get me Harris.' The operator must have had the link ready for there was no delay. I supposed there would be scrambling devices in use. Leighton picked up the mike.

'Harris, Leighton here. Bring the girl back to Carradale House straight away. I'll send the *Kestrel* over to Fairlie for you. Understood.'

'Understood.'

'Right. Over and out.'

He handed the mike back to the operator and returned to his seat. Into the phone he asked: 'You heard?'

'Yes.' I felt my mouth dry.

'You're playing out of your league, Arnott. You give too much away. Let me spell it out for you.'

'Do.'

'Firstly, we intend to get Marshall's invention come hell or high water. Secondly, we cannot afford to trust you. Nothing personal, you understand. Thirdly, we are calling the shots, not you.' His mouth twisted. 'You have shown too great an interest in Miss Stewart to let yourself be responsible for anything happening to her. Fourthly, unless you give us the timescope, Miss Stewart will be disposed of.' He shook his head slowly. 'And believe me, Arnott, you won't enjoy watching it on the 'scope.'

He paused, something implacable and repellent in his face. 'So, you will bring the plans and the prototype down to Carradale House by the first available boat. Then, if all is well, we will let you and Miss Stewart go. But if not, if it is the last thing I do, I'll kill you both. Believe me.'

'You don't really think I'd trust you to let us go.'

'You've no choice. But look here, Arnott, be rational. When we get that device, no one can touch us; we'll be in such a dominant position nothing can stop us — certainly, we'll have nothing further to fear from you two; so why shouldn't we let you go? You cannot go to the authorities and convince them. You've no proof.' His voice lost its sweet reasonableness and hardened. 'Anyway that's neither here nor there. You get down here p.d.q. with those things if you want Miss

144

Stewart to remain alive.' He looked at his watch. 'I don't suppose you can make the morning boat now. We're on the winter timetable now, so we'll expect you here at the latest half an hour after the ferry gets in at seven fifteen p.m. In fact we can come and get you at the boat.'

'No you won't,' I said sharply. 'I'll get to Carradale House by myself. And remember, when you hang up that phone you won't have broken communication with me. At least, I will still be able to see, and hear, you.' He didn't like that. I hammered home the point. 'From now on, I'll be watching and checking. You see, the prototype is battery-operated and therefore portable. So don't plan any ambushes on the road. And make sure Miss Stewart is brought to Carradale House and kept unharmed or else you've lost the timescope for ever. Oh, and one more thing. Don't think you can evade surveillance by splitting up into widely-separated groups for planning anything. I can quite easily monitor all your space-time paths using a sampling technique. And in any case, I shall be taking precautions.'

I replaced the receiver before he could ask me any further questions. I hoped he could think of some precautions that I could take. Wiping my brow, I watched the timescope's screen. Leighton, his face grim, listened for some five seconds before hanging up. Monty frowned down at him.

'Why not put me in the picture, Kenneth?'

The unconscious irony of his companion's words goaded Leighton to his feet. He opened his mouth, closed it, then laughed jerkily.

'That, as you'll have gathered, was Arnott. He will be joining us later, bringing the device we have been looking for.' He waved a hand. 'In exchange for Miss Stewart's life.'

Monty, with honest villainy, laughed. 'And we finish them off at our leisure afterwards. . . . '

Leighton smiled indulgently. 'I understand how you feel, Monty, but there's no need to take unnecessary risks. Once we have this device ISGAR will be absolutely unbeatable. We can afford to let them go. They haven't a scrap of proof.' He turned away before Monty, in his simple amazement, could blurt out anything more. 'Now I must go and have a word with Margaret. Take over here.'

I followed him upstairs. Once in his office with Miss Cornelius,

Leighton talked more freely. It was interesting to see the way she appeared to shrink and look older when he pointed out that I probably had the prototype overlooking them at that moment. It was illuminating too, the touch of cruelty in his expression as he watched her reaction. In her own peaches and cream way, however, she was tough. Recovering herself, she returned a few carefully neutral comments that indicated her agreement without disclosing any doubt as to his real intentions.

With an effort, I switched off, for although I would have given much to see Claire arrive safely and check on what was happening at Carradale House, I had no time to spare if I wanted to make that boat.

The journey across was a nightmare of impatience, fear and doubt. The weather was deteriorating fast, working up a gale when I drove on to the *Glen Sannox*. This time I stayed in the car downstairs, my eyes drawn at intervals to the package beside me while I wished I hadn't been lying when I'd told Leighton the timescope was battery-operated. The heaving ferry seemed to take aeons to reach Brodick Pier and when it did, it must have taken a good ten minutes to tie up. Once off the pierhead I wasn't at all surprised to see in the rear mirror a Zephyr Six fall in behind me.

The village was passed; I turned the Austin 1100 I had hired through the rain up the String Road, my escort following a hundred yards behind. I remembered the last time I had come up the String with Claire beside me and the way the headlamps had been reflected in the eyes of the sheep. Then I had wanted the journey to last; now I was anxious to reach my destination.

The String descended. At the sandstone pillar box I turned right, crossed Glaister Bridge and followed the twisting road over the sodden Moor to the coast at Machrie. The clicking windscreen wipers just about coped with the lashing rain. When I finally drove the Austin 1100 into the wooded grounds of Carradale House the old familiar screwed-up sick feeling of tension gripped my stomach and the driving wheel felt greasy with sweat. I stopped the car in front of the pillared portico, switched off lights and ignition and drew on the brake. In the rear mirror I saw the Zephyr draw in behind me. Nerving myself, I opened the door and got out, cold drops of rain whipped into my face by the wind. Moving round the off-side, I opened that door and lifted out the heavy package. Even with the rope round it, it was not too convenient to carry.

Slamming the door, I found the two men from the Zephyr standing at the rear of the 1100. One of them was my old friend Tee-shirt; the other I hadn't seen before. They stared carefully at me as if I was a large dog of uncertain temper. I smiled, walked round the bonnet of the Austin and up the steps. The two men fell in behind me. Ahead of me the door opened and I went inside, warm, dry air wrapping round me like a bath towel. Leighton and Miss Cornelius, with another man I didn't recognise, stood at the foot of the white marble staircase. I wondered if all the guests were confined to their rooms; on a night like this they could hardly be out on health-giving walks. I met Leighton's eyes and knew, if I'd ever doubted it, that he had no intention of letting me live a moment longer than necessary. Even across the length of the hall I could sense the hatred he felt towards me, fed by the barbs I had set in his sides during the past two days. By the same token I knew Claire's life would be cut short. Then his gaze flicked to the rain-streaked package I held and for a moment his features blazed with exultation before caution reasserted itself, schooling his face into its normal expression.

'Was he followed?'

Behind me, Tee-shirt replied. 'No, sir.'

I stepped forward, trying to look more confident than I felt.

'I take it you do not wish us to have our discussion in the hall. And if you could ask one of your minions to carry this thing; it's heavier than it looks.' With that I handed it over one-handed to Tee-shirt who underestimated its weight and almost dropped it. Leighton's face darkened.

'Come upstairs to my rooms, Arnott. Bring the package.'

We trudged upstairs, along the carpeted corridor and into the sitting-room of Leighton's suite. Once through the door I felt a surge of irrational relief when I saw Claire sitting in the same armchair I had used two nights before. She appeared pale but unharmed. Standing opposite her in the role of watchdog was Monty. When she saw me, dismay verging on despair flooded her face and she jumped up. She

147

would have run towards me if Monty hadn't gripped her arm. Leighton, still watchful, crossed to the fireplace, turned and faced us all.

'Blake and Dorman, just make sure Dr. Arnott isn't armed.'

Putting on his suave, man-of-power persona, I thought as I was seized and searched, the contents of my pockets being thrown on to the small round table in the centre of the room. Monty pawed through wallet, keys, the packet of papers, pen and pencil, diary, coins, handkerchief then tepped back.

'Nothing,' he said.

'May I?' I indicated my possessions.

'Leave them there!'

'Very well. I do assure you the keys don't explode, the pen doesn't fire tiny, steel-jacketed bullets or a jet of poison gas.' Which was a pity, I thought.

'Leave them there.' Leighton compressed his lips. 'Marshall's papers. You have them?'

I nodded towards the long envelope on the table.

'There they are.' I avoided Claire's eyes, shadowed pools of misery. Leighton strode to the table, picked up the packet, shot one sharp glance at me before returning to his former position. Eagerly he ripped open the envelope and extracted the papers. While he read, Miss Cornelius, trim in the dark suit she had worn the first time I had visited Carradale House, tried to interpret his facial expression. Monty kept his eyes on me, as did the others. I watched Leighton's face as he scanned the sheets, slipping each one behind the others as he finished with it. I was sure he would find them heavy going, all but the summary, the introduction and perhaps the occasional paragraph here and there. But in any case he wasn't in the least interested in Johnny's elaboration and development of the Benezra-Tsien theory; he wanted the timescope and the power it would give ISGAR. He read the last sheet and let his arm drop to his side. He isn't sure, I thought; he thinks it looks all right but he can't be sure.

'Right,' he said. 'Arnott, go across and stand beside Miss Stewart.' I did as I was told. I gave one side-glance at Claire then quickly looked away, unable to bear the expression in her eyes. As I expected,

Leighton dismissed the three men. Once they had left the room, undoubtedly to stand guard outside, he addressed the others.

'Monty, would you stand by the door? Thank you. Margaret, perhaps you would unwrap the package.'

So Monty's in the big secret now. He stood with his back against the oak door, right hand in his pocket. Miss Cornelius, rather gingerly, I thought, began to untie the knots in the rope binding the parcel. Beside me I felt Claire tense. The rope was finally unfastened and the wrappings were removed to reveal the timescope, its flex wound round it. Claire's exclamation was almost a sob.

'Oh Roger, no, no!'

Leighton glanced at her, obviously satisfied that her outburst was evidence that I had delivered the goods. Then he spotted the flex. His eyes raked my face.

'You said it was portable — ?'

I shrugged. 'I'm afraid I misled you, Leighton. It requires the usual household supply.'

Above the clipped moustache and neat, pointed, grey-flecked beard, his eyes seemed pale and luminous; although his expression didn't change I could see the Arnott account tally in his brain increased by one more notch. And then for a second I thought I detected relief in his face though in my tensed-up state I couldn't be sure. The moment passed. He stepped forward and walked round the timescope, examining it from all angles without touching it.

'Well,' he said, 'I think a little demonstration is necessary, just to make sure the goods are undamaged. Arnott, I wonder if you would be so kind.' His teeth gleamed momentarily as he stepped back a pace.

I walked slowly across to the timescope and unwound the flex. I looked round for a power-point. Leighton impatiently pointed to the foot of the small table that still carried the tape-recorder.

'That one,' he snapped.

I bent down, unplugged the Grundig and saw that the socket in the skirting-board was square pin. No delay there, I thought bleakly, and pushed home the timescope's plug. Leighton's eyes searched my face.

'All right. To avoid wasting time we'll take this room, two nights ago, at, say, ten p.m.' He bent his head, concentrating on every move I

149

made. When I zeroed the dials and switched on, the scene that appeared was immediately recognisable as the room we occupied. Claire, Monty and the half of the room that included the fireplace were depicted on the screen as if the timescope was a monitor receiving the signal from a TV camera somewhere in the room. I looked aside at Leighton. He nodded, his eyes glistening, his forefinger rubbing his moustache.

'Present time, present place,' I murmured.

Leighton's attention returned to me. 'Go on,' he urged.

I turned the day-dial until the second fiducial mark reached the zero then gently rotated the hour-dial. The kaleidoscopic flicker of black and white patterns on the screen, accompanied by snatches of meaningless noise, settled down to a clear picture and a voice.

'. . . what have you done with the letter. You wouldn't happen to have it on you, would you?' Pause. 'I believe you have. Now! Where did Marshall hide his stuff?' And my voice replying: 'I haven't the faintest idea.'

There was naked exultation in Leighton's voice when he spoke.

'All right, turn it off!'

As I did so, I managed to look at the others' faces. Horror and fear were the dominant emotions on Claire's face, not because of her position, I felt sure, but because she saw the nightmare future of a world controlled by ISGAR. And perhaps, I reflected bitterly, because it was I who had meekly delivered the instrument of that domination into Leighton's hands. The expression on Monty's face was compounded of a mixture of excitement and satisfaction — he doesn't see the implications, I thought. But Miss Cornelius does. Behind her impassive features, in the quick look she gave Leighton, I detected fear. I straightened up. Quite unexpectedly Leighton frowned.

'Yes. . . that seems quite satisfactory. But it reminds me of something. How did you and Marshall circumvent the truth drug?'

I hesitated. The moment's silence was broken by a window rattling under the impact of a sheet of rain. Force eight, I thought dismally.

'It's very simple,' I replied. I told him, describing how Claire and I had gone to Boquhan to retrieve the timescope from under the model in Johnny's garden. He listened without interruption. When I had finished, he nodded.

'Of course. The mistake we all made was to assume that Marshall took his work to Arran with him.' He smiled. 'Still, that doesn't matter now. The timescope does away with the need to use the truth drug.' He paused, his eyes flicking from my face to Claire's. 'We don't even need you two any more.'

'But you mean to let us go?' I queried, Simple Simon to the last.

He sniffed, his head tilting back a fraction.

'You don't seriously expect me to believe you're as naive as that, Arnott?'

'But you pointed out yourself we can't do any harm now.'

He turned on his heel, crossed to stand with his back to the fire, feet planted firmly apart, squire-fashion.

'That is true — but not in the way you thought.' Sincere indignation flooded his voice. 'You tried to doublecross me, Arnott, and that is something I will not permit.' I held my breath, my heart pounding, an overwhelming impression of final disaster looming over me. I tried to keep my voice calm and inject a note of honest bewilderment into it.

'I just do not know what you mean, Leighton. I brought you the timescope, in working order,' my hand indicated it, 'and the papers. If I did, you promised — '

'Shut up!'

I shut up. Out of the corner of my eye I saw puzzlement on Claire's face. I stole a glance at Monty. His grin was wider. He knows, I thought. Leighton's voice was even again.

'This afternoon at Glasgow University you xerographed copies of Marshall's papers. Two dozen to be exact. You meant those copies to be airmailed to two dozen of your colleagues scattered all over the world. You thought that by the time we got on to this, it would be impossible to intercept those letters. And that at least some of your colleagues would build timescopes for themselves, or tell their friends. And so the timescope would have become common property. I am quite sure you decided to use this way not only to prevent us stopping word going out, but also to ensure that no one nation would get the timescope.' He rubbed his hands slowly. 'In this way, also, ISGAR would be sure to be defeated.'

I said nothing.

'You didn't really believe we would let you go. Of course you had to come down here because there was a faint chance we would be softheaded enough to be persuaded to release Miss Stewart. But that wasn't the main reason. You came down here to buy time — time to let those letters get well on their way. That's why you've been so co-operative.' He shook his head. 'What a pity it's all been for nothing.' Another pause. He dearly loves to milk the drama from every situation, I thought.

'The letters *were* intercepted,' said Leighton. 'I had a phone call from the person who managed to achieve this. I must say that for a time I was worried in case you were watching but I soon realised that even with the timescope you had no method of tracing the call.'

'Who?' My voice shook.

The door leading to the dining-room opened.

'I'm sincerely sorry about all this, Roger, I really am.'

His halo of white hair belying the expression in the ice-blue eyes, Sir Mark Douglas-Forrest entered the room. Claire, who did not know him, looked dully at him. I probably looked like the idiot I felt.

I once saw in slow motion what happened when a bolt was thrown into the air intake of a jet engine running at top speed. For a long moment nothing happened and there was no change in the engine's scream; then the gleaming jet engine hiccoughed, its sides heaving outwards and inwards. After that it simply disintegrated, exploding and imploding all at once in a fearful sequence that ended with its complete destruction. I felt rather like that engine. All sorts of mental processes whirled on inside my head, disbelief, shock, wild truncated attempts to recompute the situation with the new factor taken into account, bitter anger at the way I had dutifully done as the Old Man had suggested, trotting about as he directed, reporting back to him whenever I could. 'Do you know what John was working on?' 'Go and see Laura.' 'Yes, I do think you should visit Machrie and see if you can find out anything.' And finally: 'The most sensible course of action we

152

can take now is to close the file and simply remember him as we all knew him — a first-rate scientist and a good man.' Epitaph for Johnny.

I felt sick and was conscious that my face must be fish-belly white. The palms of my hands felt clammy. Sir Mark said gently, as if he could read my thoughts: 'You remember I once said I considered Johnny's death an appalling waste. I meant that, Roger. I would have given a lot to keep him alive, to fit him into ISGAR, but unfortunately it wasn't possible.' He ran a hand through his white hair in that vague gesture that was so misleading. 'As it is, it looks as if you will have to go, too, and this young lady.' He smiled benignly at Claire. I managed to find my tongue.

'How long have you been in this ?'

'Many years now. I happen to be one of the four controllers of ISGAR in Britain. In fact, I suppose I entered ISGAR before you were born. You see, Roger, I survived the first war unscathed though I spent two years in the trenches. But in my possession is a rather faded photograph of my friends and contemporaries at university. Very few of them survived and of those who did, many were mutilated wrecks. And then, quite soon afterwards, we found it had all been a hideous cosmic joke for the same idiots who had let us into it had thrown away all we had fought for. So I joined ISGAR.'

'I don't like your methods.'

'Nor do I, at times. But we believe them to be necessary. We believe ISGAR must succeed.' He paused. 'Look around you, Roger, at the world we live in. A human race still breeding like rabbits although it knows full well the disastrous consequences; western man obsessionally engaged in squandering the planet's natural resources in planned obsolescence — more and more cars, tinned goods, elaborately-packed foodstuffs, beauty parlours for dogs and cats while half the world starves.

'Apart from that, our so-called scientific and affluent western civilisation has indulged in a blind use of pesticides that upsets the balance of nature, it has polluted rivers beyond recovery, poisoned the atmosphere and damaged our descendants by fall-out from criminally irresponsible nuclear tests; stockpiled atomic weapons to beyond the 'overkill' point; gone for the worship of the worthless and ephemeral while the shortage of doctors and teachers, better houses and schools actually increases; all the old moral values have been pushed aside, courage, self-sacrifice, hard work being merely snigger-worthy; religion an irrelevance or a laughing stock with a proportion of its own leaders saying "God is dead" while others try to get with it with pop masses and other circuses. Not to mention clutching at straws such as astrology or drug-taking, experimentation with psychedelics — instant mysticism, no spiritual sweat required, let's all join saints anonymous. And overall, we see the impotence of UNO and the meaningless posturings of politicians unaware that their incantations, if they ever had meaning, don't even begin to approach a solution to our problem.' He shrugged. 'I don't see any other result but disaster unless a rigid and quite ruthless control is clamped on mankind.'

I knew he was right even as I knew he was terribly wrong; I could even see how someone like him could join an organisation like ISGAR and persuade himself as so many have done before him that the end justifies the means. But have to keep persuading himself again and again. Which reminded me.

'I take it, then, that you'll get rid of us.'

Again that so-misleading gesture, that impression of not being quite *au fait* with the situation.

'I'm afraid so, my boy. You've had a good run for your money and you very nearly managed it. It was quite an ingenious idea getting Anne to stick those copies into envelopes and asking her to put the first two dozen names on your address list on them. Unfortunately I had already told her I was seriously worried about you and that I'd like to be told about anything you might do. So the child simply brought them to me for my okay before she sent them out.' He smiled. 'Anyway, I phoned Leighton this afternoon and he sent the *Kestrel* over for me. Shocking journey. I thought I'd better be here since matters were obviously approaching a climax.'

Partly from curiosity, partly to spin things out, I asked:

'How did you find out Johnny had invented the timescope?'

'That was a bit of luck. He came to see me in my room, told me about this new discovery he had made and how he'd like to get away for a few days to assess it. He was under such an intense strain that my interest

154

was aroused. "I can't tell you anything about it at the moment," he said. "It certainly works — that's not the problem. It's just that it mustn't fall into the wrong hands of any group of men, official or unofficial; it'd give them world power. And yet, I'm not sure that it should be in the public's possession either — it could lead to the breakdown of our civilisation." ' Sir Mark shrugged. 'After that I knew we had to get it — especially since I held Johnny's capabilities in high esteem. So I contacted Leighton here — it was again fortunate that of the six centres we have in Scotland, one was situated in Arran.' He tilted his head slightly. 'I think you know the rest.'

'Yes,' I said. 'You murdered him as surely as if you had broken his neck yourself.' I inhaled deeply. 'May I ask how you intend to get rid of us?'

He looked at Leighton.

'What had you in mind, Kenneth?'

'Oh, we'll take them out in the *Kestrel* and drop them overboard with chains padlocked round them. They'll never be found.' He grinned. 'And I suggest the sooner the better, before this storm blows itself out. Agreed, Sir Mark? We have a working timescope and plans. We don't need them any more.'

I was no longer listening, at least not to those in the room. For the past hour, all through my bid to spin out the proceedings as long as I could, I had been straining to detect anything above the intermittent voice of the wind and the lead shot-like battering the rain was giving the curtained window. And now I heard something. Two muffled shouts through the thick door that Monty guarded. Then five shots in quick succession. A scrabbling at the door. Another shout. Monty whipped the door open. Tee-shirt, three crimson splashes across his chest, fell through, mouth agape. Monty glanced into the corridor, half-sobbed and tried to slam the door. Tee-shirt's body, sprawled half-across the threshold, wedged it open. Monty whimpered in frustration. More shouts and the thud of running feet. Monty whirled, tugging at the gun in his pocket, his eyes white-circled with fear. The door crashed back. Two figures in wet, camouflaged denims, sten guns at the ready, catapulted through. Monty stumbled backwards, lost his balance and thudded down on his back, his automatic pistol skidding

155

over the thick carpet to my feet. The two sten guns, two black sides of a right angle, covered the room. One of the intruders snapped, in quick, Cockney accents: 'Be very still, everyone'.

Tableaux. Even Monty, mouth open, had frozen like one of those twisted plaster figures dug out of the lava of ancient Pompeii. The lightning sequence of events had probably taken less than eight seconds in all, I thought, my eyes on Leighton's thunderstruck face. Two more isolated shots sounded from somewhere outside. Two more men entered the room, one wearing a black oilskin over civvies, the other in denims, a crown glinting on each shoulder. I grinned at the civilian.

'Hello, George, you're late. What kept you?'

George, his bluff, shiny anxious face relaxing, grinned back, his shoulders heaving as he gulped air. The hard-looking major looked at me, a machine pistol slung from one shoulder.

'Dr. Arnott?'

'Yes.'

'Major Prebble, Second Strike Group, Parachute Regiment. My men have now taken charge of Carradale House. Other groups are on their way.' His eyes swept the room. 'I'm afraid weather conditions delayed our arrival. And we thought it best to land the helicopters on the edge of the Moor rather than to try to put them down inside the glen. Gave us quite a spring.' He looked at the timescope. 'I take it this is what we have to take charge of. Now, sir, would you be so kind as to identify your companions?' As he spoke, a sergeant arrived, saluted and announced, 'Takeover complete, sir. Two of ours wounded, not seriously; three of them dead, including this one, I think.' Prebble dismissed him and returned his attention to me. I took my cue.

'ISGAR members: Monty, on the floor there; Miss Cornelius, by the window; Leighton and Sir Mark Douglas-Forrest.' Miss Cornelius stood, her pale features impassive; Leighton, beside Claire, still appeared stunned and disbelieving; the Old Man's face was stony and somehow crumpled. To my surprise I felt a completely irrational surge of regret within me. Bang goes one father-figure, I thought.

'Yes, George,' I heard myself saying in reply to his audible gasp, 'I'm afraid Sir Mark is one of them.' I drew a deep breath. 'And major, this is Miss Stewart, definitely one of us.'

Leighton's voice was flat and dead. Only his eyes retained life.

'How did you do it, Arnott?'

'I phoned George at the Department, got him to come to me as quickly as possible. After demonstrating the timescope, I explained the situation to him, very quickly convincing him by using the timescope to illustrate parts of my story. Being also an electronics genius — ' I noticed George smirk modestly ' — he readily made sense of Dr. Marshall's circuit diagrams. When I further emphasised the desperate urgency of the matter and how I had to bring the timescope down here, he set to work to build another. With it and a copy of the papers, he went to the authorities. He is quite high up in Civil Defence and therefore knew the right people to go to. Tell me, George, how long did it take to build another timescope?'

'Just under three hours. Using the Department radiation detector helped a lot and it was a bit of a lash-up but it worked. I had no real difficulty convincing security once I showed them scenes from their childhood and a few matters they considered to be top secret.'

Leighton nodded. Sir Mark looked strangely at me.

'So you've lost after all, Roger.'

I knew what he meant; so did Claire, judging by the far from happy expression on her face. The Old Man spoke gently, elaborating his statement.

'If I hadn't intercepted those letters you planned to send abroad, timescanning would have become common knowledge; as it is, the War Office and MI5 will hang on to it, hugging it to themselves as their top secret weapon, the weapon that gives them access to every foreign secret weapon in existence, access to every secret conference, every suspect's life. What power!' He shook his head. 'Too bad, Roger, too bad.'

I never learned if he meant to say more. Leighton moved. With one leap he was behind Claire, his arm round her waist, his right hand pointing a shiny-black pistol at her head. The nearer paratrooper jerked over his sten but somehow managed to avoid pulling the trigger.

I felt the itch of sweat on my forehead. Leighton, his eyes glaring, his lips parted, shouted at us:

'Don't move, anyone!'

Sir Mark frowned, as if in exasperation at a shocking display of bad taste.

'Don't be a fool, Kenneth, it's all over.'

Leighton's head jerked. 'Not for me. Margaret, are you coming?'

'Where to?' Miss Cornelius's dull tones displayed complete awareness of the fact that in the two hundred million square miles the world offered, there did not exist a single hiding place the timescope could not find, be it deep in the jungle of the Matto Grosso, or tucked away in the most inconspicuous house in the world's largest city. But Leighton seemed beyond rational appreciation of the situation. To have the world snatched from him at the fifty-ninth minute of the eleventh hour was too much. He addressed the major.

'I am walking out of here. Once out of the House I will shoot Miss Stewart if anyone comes after me.'

I was hypersensitively aware of the gun touching my foot, of my inability to get to it in time, even if I could have hit Leighton, of Major Prebble's razor-edge of indecision. I prayed that no one would try to be heroic or do his duty.

'Let him go, Major,' I said quietly. 'It's not important.'

Leighton's eyes held mine.

'Pick up that timescope and smash it, Arnott. Go on,' he urged, 'do as I say.' A sudden movement of his hand thrust the pistol muzzle against the side of Claire's head; with a gasp of pain she jerked her head to one side; the pistol followed it. I pulled the input plug from its socket, lifted the timescope and threw it to the floor. A loud thud mingled with the crash, telling me the tube had imploded. He's gambling on the other timescope being out of range, I thought dully, or of him getting beyond its range. But it's not going to do him any good — he's reacting like a trapped animal.

Leighton pushed Claire forward. 'Everyone keep well back. Major, go ahead and tell your men to let us through. Go!' He flicked a glance at me. 'You're coming, too, Arnott. Pick the ignition key off the table.'

I did so. The paratroop major, his jaw muscles rigid with anger, backed out of the room. I preceded Claire and Leighton out of the door, along the panelled corridor to the top of the staircase. By that time the major was half-way down the marble treads, ordering the half-dozen armed paratroopers standing in the hall below to let us pass. Slowly I descended the curved staircase, the faces of the denim-covered men below turned up to me, chessmen set out in some end game on the gleaming black and white tiled floor. I found myself breathing through my mouth. At the foot of the stairs, Leighton spoke again, his voice a tone above its usual pitch.

'Even if I am shot, I can still press the trigger. Open the door, Arnott. Go out and open the near side back seat door of your car. Then stand back at least ten feet. When Miss Stewart and I are inside and I have closed the door, take your place at the wheel. Do you understand?'

'Yes.'

Down the steps. The rain is almost off now; the wind is falling. Open the rear door. Back ten paces into the darkness. Watch Leighton and Claire, spotlighted by the yellow shaft of light from the vestibule, enter the Austin 1100, the gun still pressed against her head. Crunch of pebbles as you approach the driver's door. Open it, sit in, swing your legs in, neck prickling at the tangible aura of menace from the dark behind you. Fire the engine, use floor change to put the car in first. Release brake: take the cold wheel and allow the clutch to come up slowly. Put on sides and headlights.

'Dip those headlights, Arnott. Go straight down to the harbour. We're boarding the *Kestrel*.'

Useless to reason with him, to point out he's only borrowing a little time before the timescope, sweeping along his life-path, brings inevitable capture.

The car sped down the curved driveway, the headlights splashing light off bushes and trees. The gateway, a black rectangular gap, appeared. I slowed down between the gateposts, cast a glance right then left and swung the car on to the main road. Ten yards along, I saw the opening leading on to the short cart-track to the harbour and swung right. We bounced down the rutted track. He'll go on board with Claire, get me to cast off then shoot me. Claire next. Fighting the bucketing car, I tried to visualise the little harbour from boyhood memory. We rattled on to the stony surface at twenty miles an hour, I snapped back into first gear, rammed my foot down on the accelerator and shouted despairingly:

'Hold on! We're going over!'

The car leaped forwards, engine racing, shot over the far end of the harbour at forty miles an hour and dropped in a stomach-jerking paraboloidal plunge that grabbed Leighton's mind until we hit water, bonnet first. Even prepared and braced for it, the thud with which my body met the wheel almost caused me to pass out. Amid the crash of water, the heaving roll of the almost submerged car back to the surface, the darkness and disorientation, I twisted round, sobbing as a flame of agony seared my ribs. In the faint greenish dashboard light I saw Leighton, gun still in hand, sprawled over the back seat. I grabbed his gun arm and pulled it forward and down. The gun went off so close to my ear that I felt as if it had been struck by a hammer. An icy, heavy inrush of water over head and shoulders followed the shattering of the side window by the bullet. Claire shouted: 'Roger — are you all right?'; Leighton tugged frenziedly at me while the freezingly cold sea-water rose swiftly about my knees and thighs to my waist.

The car lurched. I finally bashed the gun from Leighton's hand and pushed him away as a heaving wall of water submerged my head. A red-hot band of iron compressed my chest as I felt for the door-handle. Pressures being almost equalised by now, the door opened easily. I pushed myself out, holding on to the door post and found the rear door open. In the total blackness someone clung to me and we thrust our way upwards. With a gasp, I broke the surface and stared at my companion. It was Claire. Half-laughing, half-sobbing, the cold, salt taste of sea-water entering our mouths, we kissed and clung together. A cone of light from a powerful torch held by someone up on the harbour spotlighted us. I looked around. Bubbles still fizzed up over the place where the car lay submerged. There was no trace of Leighton.

We swam slowly along the foot of the harbour wall past the *Kestrel* to the stone steps where two of the paratroopers stood to help us out. The stabbing pain that hit me as I was pulled from the water told me that at least one rib had gone. In addition, my right ear still roared, the aftermath of the gunshot. And, I realised hysterically, my blistered feet stung. I looked up at Claire and laughed then wished I hadn't.

They had commandeered the Land Rover. In it, we drove back to the road, a sergeant and two men being left to cover the *Kestrel.* The rain had stopped. The wet road gleamed among the shadowy undergrowth of whin; the sides of the mountains girdling the glen raised themselves up to a black skyline where dark, broken clouds raced over the summit as if eager to blot out the moon. Down to the right, the sea imitated all moonlit seas after a storm, with waves pounding whitely on the wet shingle, pushing at a black ragged line of seaweed. My eyes burned with the salt water and I sensed how near to complete exhaustion I was. As the Land Rover turned into the gateway of the House, my sodden clothes tugged at my body.

I looked at my watch. If it was still going, it was eight-fifteen. We clambered out of the Land Rover and entered Carradale House, almost every window now brightly lit. In the hall the major grinned at us.

'You'd better find dry togs. I suggest you ransack Leighton's rooms and, what's her name, Miss Cornelius's. They owe it to you. I'll be up to see you later. Still one or two things to attend to.'

We nodded. I glanced at the grandfather clock standing by the oak settle. Eight-seventeen. I tried to breathe as shallowly as possible.

'Let's go to Leighton's sitting-room first, Claire, there's something I must see.'

She looked enquiringly at me, her salt-sticky dark hair clinging to her head. I thought she looked marvellous. I smiled. We climbed the stairs, went along the corridor and pushed open the door. It seemed like a mile to me. The others were still seated now in a row of chairs against the wall facing us. On our side stood the two paratroopers. The latter flicked glances at us, grinned happily, then resumed their watch. George, now out of his oilskin, turned back from the window he had been peering through, his plump face jubilant under the pepper and salt crew cut.

'Am I glad to see you two! Where's Leighton?'

'Dead,' I said shortly, noting the almost complete lack of reaction from Monty and Miss Cornelius. I thought I didn't imagine the slight

161

warmth in Sir Mark's eyes. Yet he'd have had us killed, I marvelled. For a moment our eyes met before I crossed to the large TV set. I switched it on.

'Some light entertainment while you wait.'

I stepped back to stand beside Claire in front of the fire. The heat began to penetrate my clothes. The screen lit up, showing the earnest Harold Lloyd features of Clark Desmond.

'. . . surely in importance rivals the splitting of the atom or the discovery of the antibiotics in its ultimate effect on our daily life. Perhaps posterity will remember the twentieth century not as the century men first landed on the moon, but the century when John Stanhope Marshall invented the timescope. It is too early yet to list all the multifarious ways in which this incredible invention can be applied. Every time I think about it, some new application springs to mind.'

He continued along ground familiar to us, describing how historical research and archaeology could become sciences, the possible far-reaching effects on religious faith; how police would benefit, for example in tracing missing children, solving crimes; how crime statistics would fall with the knowledge that capture and retribution were inevitable. 'The invention may well be the last chance man has of growing up, of sweeping away all the lies and hypocrisies in international life that hinder the understanding of nation by nation, prevent disarmament conferences reaching agreement because of fear and mistrust and mutual suspicion. No one group of men will be able to blind their fellows by propaganda; there is no place for Dr. Goebbels in the world of the timescope; the credibility gap between government and governed becomes exactly calibrated when the man in the street can turn to his own timescope and see for himself.'

He paused. I flicked a weary glance round the hypnotised room (talk about a captive audience) and returned my gaze to the screen.

'In the Concise Oxford Dictionary, the word "deadlight" is defined as a shutter protecting a cabin window or porthole in a storm. Perhaps this invention that lights up the past is in more than one sense a deadlight. Perhaps in a very real sense it will protect the human race from the storm of nuclear and bacteriological warfare that has threatened it for over twenty years. I certainly hope so.

162

'And now, let me introduce Dr. Roger Arnott, of the Department of Cybernetic Studies, Glasgow University, a colleague of Dr. Marshall's. After the latter's tragic death, Dr. Arnott collected his papers and prototype apparatus. In fact the first working timescope is here in the studio now with Dr. Marshall's colleague to explain its principles and demonstrate its use.'

The camera swung to show the original timescope, the one I had smashed a quarter of an hour ago. Behind me, blown up sheets of circuit diagrams pinned to boards were clearly visible. I watched my other self indicating parts of the design, using the diagrams to explain Johnny's ideas, talking of the range of the first timescope and finally drawing out of the past eighty years moving pictures from where no movie camera had ever been. As I watched, I had a sudden vision of the television transmitter punching its signal up through earth's atmosphere, beyond the D, E and F layers of the ionosphere, twenty thousand miles out into space to where the stationary communications satellite received it and relayed it through other satellites back to receivers scattered over most of the earth's surface. And in scores of places, in a dozen or more nations, the programme would be being taped and by tomorrow, radio hams, electronic engineers, amateur and professional, in civil and military laboratories, or in their own homes, would have begun timescanning. Bigger and better timescopes would be built. It would be a snowball no one could stop. For better or for worse, the truth would be part of mankind's life from now on.

I switched off. The square of light flashed to a bright point, lingered and vanished.

'After I saw you, George, I went to see Clark Desmond at the Caledonian TV studios. I convinced him of the timescope's staggering potentialities and that it shouldn't become the property of any one group or nation. You may recall that Desmond in his earlier years had a lot to do with Ban the Bomb marchers and people of similar sympathies.' I sighed and winced. 'It also helped him to decide to throw out his scheduled programme and substitute the taped one he did with me when I revealed that I had already posted two dozen letters spilling the beans and that this was his one chance to beat the field.'

163

I turned to Claire. 'Shall we go and try to find some dry clothes?'
Outside the room, in the long corridor, she looked at me.

'You're going to be very unpopular in certain quarters, Roger.'

'Yes,' I replied quietly. All at once I felt desperately tired and not a bit triumphant. She stood facing me. Over her shoulder the corridor window disclosed the now peaceful scene, courtyard, stables, garden, grounds and woods. Storm's over: next one is scheduled to begin any time now. Casualties are expected to be heavy. From my exhausted mind appeared a rapid series of hypnagogic images, episodic, unbidden, consequences of my actions. I saw the faces of men and women, old and young, whose faith I had destroyed, the angry gobbling features of the politicians I had made buffoons and liars of, the blank unknown features of lawbreakers, major and minor, legal and moral, from whom I had swept security. There was no order in the succession. The people from whom I had taken life were mixed with the faces of sadists and pornographers to whom I had given an inexhaustible supply of stimuli. I thought of ancient historical mysteries solved, of cavemen and mammoths and pterodactyls and primitive rain-soaked forests. I saw Johnny, grinning ruefully while Laura wept and wondered if he would have approved.

Claire watched my face.

'There's no going back now, Roger.' She put a hand on my arm. 'And I wouldn't worry too much. I think the human race will weather the storm.'

I hoped so.

'ISGAR is finished,' I said. Claire nodded.

'That is certainly true.' She looked sideways at me, her long thick lashes screening her eyes. 'One way or another, you've finished quite a lot of things, including my work. Tricky devil, aren't you?'

'Only when I'm pushed.'

'I shall have to remember that, shan't I?' She smiled slowly, the sparkle in her eyes repeating the promise she had once made me and I began to feel much improved. Somehow the future, though still enigmatic, didn't look so bad.